the
Sweetest
Sound

the Sweetest Sound

a novel by

SHERRI WINSTON

LITTLE, BROWN AND COMPANY
New York Boston

Little, Brown and Company
Hachette Book Group
1290 Avenue of the Americas, New York, NY 10104
Visit us at LBYR.com

Originally published in hardcover and ebook by Little, Brown and Company in January 2017
First Trade Paperback Edition: January 2018

The Library of Congress has cataloged the hardcover edition as follows:

Names: Winston, Sherri, author.
Title: The sweetest sound / by Sherri Winston.
Description: First edition. | New York ; Boston : Little, Brown and Company, 2017. |
Summary: "Shy ten-year-old Cadence grapples with an overprotective father, a mother who's skipped town to pursue stardom, and what to do when a recording of her amazing voice leaks before she's ready to share it with the world" —Provided by publisher.
Identifiers: LCCN 2015039110 | ISBN 9780316302951 (hardcover) | ISBN 9780316302920 (ebook) | ISBN 9780316355049 (library edition ebook)
Subjects: | CYAC: Singing—Fiction. | Bashfulness—Fiction. | Mothers and daughters—Fiction. | African Americans—Fiction.
Classification: LCC PZ7.W7536 Sw 2017 | DDC [Fic]—dc23
LC record available at http://lccn.loc.gov/2015039110

ISBNs: 978-0-316-30293-7 (pbk.), 978-0-316-30292-0 (ebook)

Printed in the United States of America

LSC-C

10 9 8 7 6 5 4 3 2 1

Thank you, George and Mariah!

–S. W.

Prelude

Birthdays are a problem for me. It's been that way for almost four years. My seventh birthday was the last time life felt normal. My party was amazing. We ate dinner at a Mexican restaurant, just family and a few friends—the way I like it. One of my friends, Faith, is from the Dominican Republic, so even though people assume she's African American, she speaks Spanish quite well, thank you very much! She taught us some words. The band played "Happy Birthday to You!" the Spanish way, and we sang "*Feliz cumpleaños a ti.*" The music felt like sunshine on my skin, and Faith, Zara, and I did silly dances. My mother even sang with the band.

It was the best night. Just the absolute best!

The next morning I found a note on the coffeepot. It read:

> *I love you all so much. But I have to pursue my passion. I can't grow in Harmony, can't be a star here. Jeremiah, you are a great man, wonderful husband, and terrific father. Cadence and Junior are lucky to have you. You deserve to be loved more than I can offer. Please don't hate me. Cadence, my sweet little Mouse, so quiet and shy. Always remember, you are the high note of my life. I will always love you.*
>
> *Chantel Marie Jolly*

And then, she was gone.

Birthdays have been tricky ever since.

My name is Cadence Mariah Jolly.

I live in western Pennsylvania in a small town called Harmony.

I'm up in the middle of the night because I simply cannot sleep. Last year I stood outside my bedroom on this very balcony, staring past the dark mountaintops, pleading for a miracle. If God answered my prayers it would be a sign. No more sad, weird birthdays.

That's what I thought. Truly.

Funny thing, though. God answered my prayers. I got exactly what I wanted.

Now, four weeks away from my next birthday, that blessing feels more like a curse.

I read a book over the summer called *Holes*. It was about this kid, Stanley Yelnats, who got sent away to an awful juvie place in the desert for something he didn't even do. Talk about a curse! It was a great book, and I've reread it a few times. I plan to be a No. 1 Bestselling Author of Amazing Stories one day, so I like to study the works of other authors.

I love reading, because authors have an amazing gift—they see problems and they find solutions. Have you ever wondered how an author would fix your life in a book? If the author of *Holes*, Louis Sachar, wrote a book about me, would he write about the fact that I'm really quiet? That at times I like being alone? Would he write about how I get this shaky, dry-mouthed feeling that makes my heart race whenever I'm around a lot of people? And if he did write a story about a girl like me, one who loves to read and plans to write great stories, a girl who is quiet yet tired of getting talked over and overlooked, tired of being pitied, how would Mr. Sachar fix her? (Me?)

Trust me. I've got lots that need fixing.

All I asked God for was one thing: for Daddy to find a way to get me a Takahashi 3000x keyboard and microphone. (It's the kind used by all the best Internet sensations! At least, that's what Faith says.)

In my prayers, I promised I'd share my secret talent with the world, if only God made my dream come true. My aunt and lots of people at church were always warning us kids about our prayers. *God ain't no Santa Claus,* they liked to say. *When you talk to the Lord, be mindful of what you're asking for. A prayer is a powerful thing.*

Honest, I believe in God, but truthfully, I wasn't quite convinced He'd even care about my keyboard or my secret.

Until it happened. God granted my wish. It was like some kind of miracle.

Somehow Daddy got his hands on a busted-up Takahashi 3000x and fixed it without me finding out. Next thing you know, I get the keyboard for my birthday. A real dream come true.

Now it's time to keep my promise. But I don't think I can.

What happens if you make a promise to God, then try to take it back?

1

Underneath the Stars

Some words feel so grown-up when you say them. Like *scintillating.* I whispered the word like it was part of a magic spell. One of many astronomy terms I learned from my mother. It means twinkling like stars. When she taught it to me, she would say it, then tell me to repeat it, and touch my lips as I did. Said to let it tumble from my mouth.

My mother loved staring into the night sky. She loved pointing out groups of stars called constellations. She told me *I* loved it, too. Which was funny, because I could have sworn that staring into the sky at distant planets and glowing dust used to scare me. It made me feel so small, like I was vanishing. All I knew about the sky and the stars was what my big brother, Junior, had told me. Which was that slimy aliens and space monsters lived out there—he knew it because someone named Captain Kirk told him so. Like I knew the difference between Captain Kirk and Cap'n Crunch.

I told her once, my mother, that looking into the deep vastness of the sky made me afraid. She surprised me, saying it used to do the same to her. She said she'd wondered as a kid about the universe with all of its mysteries, but she figured its mysteriousness was part of its beauty.

She was so convinced that I loved it as much as she did that she ordered a telescope as a gift for my fifth birthday.

Don't get me wrong. I did get quite a few things that I loved, too. Such as a tiny iPod and multiple pairs of candy-colored earbuds. I love music. My favorite singer was (and still is) Mariah Carey. She is like my fairy godmother. If fairy godmothers were real, which they aren't. Except...maybe. I haven't quite figured that out. Anyway, I had listened to my Mariah playlist for so long, it was as if her songs were made to explain all the chapters of my life.

Later on, of course, my mother was gone, but the night sky no longer freaked me out. I gazed into the tiny lens of the telescope because seeing the stars up close made me feel closer to her. I knew that Captain Kirk was a make-believe character in *Star Trek*, and aliens and space monsters were make-believe, too. Probably.

I also knew that most of the time, especially lately, I was the one who felt like an alien. Staring into the heavens, I imagined stories about the planets and the moon. Outer space didn't make me feel invisible anymore; people did.

Darkness wrapped around me. I pressed my eyes shut and remembered the touch of my mother's fingertips on my skin.

When I opened my eyes, her image appeared in the sparkling mass of constellations. The shape of her face was Cassiopeia; her eyes, Polaris; the curve of her neck, the handle on the Big Dipper. Just the way I remembered her, before she left us. Beautiful and distant. *Scintillating.*

I used to get lost in the shadow of her shine. She was so beautiful and talented that it was like she cast this bright glow, you know? And the light from her amazingness reached way up into the heavens. I could never, ever come close.

When she left, our world slipped into darkness. Would it be that way forever?

♫ ♫ ♫

Our house is three stories high. The top floor is like my apartment—I have it all to myself since my mother left and Daddy said he couldn't face being up here alone. He and Junior carted all my things up from the first floor because Junior said he didn't want to be up here, either.

Now it's just me and the last wonderful gift my mother ever gave me: my floppy-eared spaniel terrier, Lyra. She'd say hi, except it's late. Really late. And Lyra loves her beauty sleep.

Holding Lyra close, I leaned back on the chair and took in the night sky. My imagination conjured a familiar story. One that absolutely, positively made me sway. The way you might if you stood up too fast and got light-headed.

The story came out of my soul, and now it rests in a journal. All good writers keep journals. When I grow up, I will write wonderful stories about girls who are brave and wise and fearless. Girls unafraid to stand out. Girls nothing like me.

So, in the story I made up, my mother is no longer absent. She's returned. She is in awe of my writing talent. She loves me so much and wishes she had not left me back when I was a little kid.

We are being interviewed on TV. The host has tears in her eyes talking about my amazing new book. She says with a name like Cadence Mariah, it's no wonder my words flow like a song, no wonder I grew up playing the piano and singing in my school and church choirs. The TV host understands. *Cadence* means "rhythm." Middle name, Mariah, as in the famous singer, Mariah Carey. (See why I feel like she's my fairy godmother?)

Now, in my story, which flashes across the purplish mountainside like in a movie on a theater screen, I see the whole scene so clearly. I'm laughing with the interviewer, a quiet little laugh, and explaining how I used to be so shy that I hid in the back rows of the choirs.

My mother, I reveal to the talk show lady, is known throughout our hometown for sounding like the famous singer Whitney Houston. When I was born, Daddy says, she couldn't bear to share the perfection of Miss Houston with me. Instead, she made my middle name the same as her second-favorite singer, Miss Mariah Carey. But to me, Miss Mariah would always be No. 1!

The TV show lady, tears glittering in her eyes, begs the two of us to sing a song together.

My mother says, *No, she couldn't.* She says, *My baby won't sing because she is so shy.*

And then the TV show lady looks at me. Eyes pleading.

I walk over to my mother. I am very confident and sophisticated. The youngest bestselling author in the whole, entire world. She does not know how much I've changed since she left us. I am different now. Not the same Mouse.

I say, *Okay, Mother. I will sing with you.* In a totally low-voiced, dramatic sort of way.

And then we stand in the middle of the stage. My mother slips her hand into mine. Then the music begins.

The orchestra knows exactly what song to play. The only song that makes sense:

"When You Believe."

It is the only duet between the great Miss Houston and the amazing Miss Mariah.

When we begin to sing, my mother stares in disbelief. She cannot believe how beautiful my voice is. She always wanted me to be a singer. Like her. But I don't think she believed it would happen. I was always too shy. Was that why she left us?

She did try to be happy as a wife and mother, working part-time at the Superstar Gas n' Grocery Mart while taking classes at the community college.

But that kind of life was making her die inside, Daddy said. He said somebody like my mother was born for bigger things. He said we did not wish her ill, but would, in fact, pray for her success and joy and happiness. Like my mother, Daddy seemed to think he knew what I was feeling without even asking. And even though my mother sent me a phone as a gift, she rarely called or left a number where I could reach her. Still, I told myself that was okay. I would hold no grudges; I told myself I forgave her. In my heart, I hoped it was true.

So, in my story, my incredible, amazing, can't-put-down, make-believe story, there we are. Reunited.

And singing.

It is the best feeling in the whole wide world.

I stared into the sky.

The stars were twinkling their applause. My heart danced in its cage. Lyra snuggled up to my ankles and let out a low doggie moan. I reached down and scruffed her neck. She was a small white dog with spots of golden and chocolate brown spattered over her face and ears. I named her after the constellation Lyra, which was itself named for an instrument played in Greek mythology.

While my mother believed in all kinds of mythology, Daddy was a man who believed in keeping his feet firmly on the ground. When he wasn't busy working for the sheriff's department as a deputy or helping with the high school football team as an assistant coach, his real love was fixing old instruments. He actually had an instrument in his shop called a lyre. It made the coolest sounds. He had something else called a lute. Sort of like an old-fashioned guitar with a potbelly. I loved the lute and begged him to teach me how to play it, so he did. He refinished one and gave it to me as a gift.

My fingers trailed across the strings of the lute now resting on my lap. A weird hollow feeling deep inside my chest made me shake inside out.

Slumping beneath the quilt thrown across my shoulders, I sank into the creaky wooden chair. Lyra stirred, then she hopped onto my lap, pushing the lute aside. The warmth of her body, the scent of her doggie shampoo, made me draw a deep, calming breath. My fingers casually strummed the belly of the handmade instrument, the notes sad and sweet like tree boughs singing in the wind.

I like to think that my mother gave me Lyra because she wanted someone here to watch over me—all of us—while she went out into the world to make her dreams come true. She was a singer, and a singer needed to sing.

So I wished her the very best. Tried to, anyway.

I breathed in air that was cold and tasted like winter, even though the calendar still said fall. It felt so peaceful. I inhaled the quiet back into my lungs.

Then the peacefulness gave way to a knocking beat in my chest. My heart skipped a scratchy, snare drum rhythm. The lute's music sounded melancholy. Another excellent grown-up word—*melancholy*. I was having trouble concentrating. Partly because of the secret I was hiding. And partly because of the promise I had yet to keep.

♫ ♫ ♫

Last year, sitting right here, I prayed and prayed for Daddy to find a way to buy me the keyboard. And I promised God I'd stop being so boring and scared and start taking chances. No. 1 Bestselling Authors of Amazing Stories get their ideas from being bold, not by hiding from EVERYTHING.

I was too shy and too scared. I did have to hand it to my mother about one thing, though—piano lessons. I started playing at three years old, and even though I still get butterflies sometimes, I know I'm pretty good.

The music teacher at school and choir director at church knew about our family. Everyone did. Funny thing having a whole town pity you. Everyone bending over backwards to "help." They tolerated my shyness. I hid behind other singers so I wouldn't throw up on anybody's shoe. But when the music teachers or directors needed me, I could play the piano or keyboard well enough to help. It worked out well for everybody.

Replacing my dinky little keyboard with a Takahashi 3000x got me singing around the house all the time. Well, when I was alone, that is. I loved how singing touched my heart and made me feel light. Powerful. Strong. I wished I had the courage to sing in front of real people.

Once I realized how good it felt, singing out loud with all my heart, mumble-singing in the back rows of the choir became more difficult. Still, I was determined not to draw attention to myself. I got enough attention for being the girl whose mother left. Everybody treated me like I was made of glass. Like I was broken.

Am I broken? Would I know it if I were?

One day Reverend Shepherd had given a sermon about

blessings. He said God has anointed each of us with special gifts and talents. He said ignoring them was a sin. He said we should stand in our blessings, which I'd figured meant if God gave you a talent, you were supposed to use it. Kind of like a superpower.

You know, church is like that. Sometimes the pastor is talking and all you can think about is eating pancakes when he is done. But sometimes he says something and, just like that, it feels like he's talking absolutely, positively to YOU. I got chills as he talked about keeping our talents a secret.

"God knows all your secrets," he'd said. I practically ducked down in my seat.

Honestly! Fear and guilt followed me like a cloud. I'd promised to use my voice to sing loud and stop being shy if He granted my wish. But I wasn't sure I was ready to do that.

Maybe I needed some kind of sign. Like when Moses struck the rock and it flowed with water in Numbers 20:10–11. Or in Matthew 14:17–21 when He fed the multitudes with loaves and fishes. I mean, in Bible School, we learned that when God gives us a sign, we need to pay attention. We understood that if you have faith, God will deliver miracles.

While I waited for a sign, I kept practicing at my piano teacher's house. Mrs. Reddit was also the music teacher at my school; she gave lessons on the side. One day while we were practicing, she had gone to make a call, and I got caught up in one of the pieces—"His Eye Is on the Sparrow"—and began to sing. The words did not get caught in my throat or stumble over my lips. They passed through my heart, one by one, until they rose up to the chandelier above the dining room table. Singing with all my soul made me feel free and beautiful and loved.

Until I finished and realized Mrs. Reddit was standing right there.

Then I felt trapped and terrified and exposed.

My heart started pounding. My face felt hot and itchy. But part of me truly also wondered if she thought I was as good as I'd begun to think I was—even though I didn't want to think about being good at all.

And sure enough, she said, "Cadence, was that really you? That was the most amazing thing, child. How long have you been singing like that?"

She saw the terror in my eyes. Saw me start to shake. She rushed over. Wrapped her long, thin arms around me. Hugged my body into her powdery perfume softness.

"Please don't tell. Please don't tell. Please don't tell," I whispered over and over again. I wasn't even sure who I thought she'd tell. I just knew I didn't want anyone else finding out.

Mrs. Reddit, being so awesome and all, promised it would be our secret. "When you're ready to sing in public, you will. I hope one day you will trust me with your gift and let me show you how to make it shine," she said.

After that, even when I was hiding in the back row of choir in her class, Mrs. Reddit never mentioned my singing again.

But now, my two best friends, Zara and Faith, were counting on me. In a little less than a month, I'd be turning eleven. An important age in choir years. At church, eleven was how old you had to be to go from the baby choir, which we were in, to the Youth Choir with the big kids. And nobody got into the Youth Choir without auditioning. In front of everyone.

Zara and Faith had already had their birthdays. Now it was up to me. We'd vowed to be ready for the next round of auditions, which were the first Thursday of the month. That meant they were a little over four weeks away, the week after my birthday. All of church's choirs would be performing in the upcoming Gospel Music Jamboree the day after Thanksgiving. And we didn't want to be stuck in the baby choir for the show.

The problem? I was still so terrified of singing in public. I was not ready.

And time was running out.

2

Emotions

A funny thing happens when people are constantly trying to fix you: Eventually, you believe you need fixing. Being everyone's favorite makeover project was simply exhausting. To me, it seemed perfectly normal to sit alone in my room and spend a whole day reading and writing, listening to music, or playing on the keyboard. Whenever I was at school or out someplace surrounded by people, after a while it made me feel tired. On weekends I could spend a whole day without wanting or needing to talk to anyone. *That* felt right.

However, according to town legend, my quietness had worried my mother from the time I was a little baby. According to that same legend, she worried that I needed to come out of my shell. I was three years old. Perfect shell size, thank you very much!

Those were the thoughts twisting inside my head on Saturday morning while working on chores with Daddy.

Not quite eight o'clock yet. Must clean, must polish, must shine.

Our routine. Junior was a late riser. He did yard work, garbage collection, wood polishing, and more, but not this early in the day.

Daddy was a former air force man. He liked order.

Saturday mornings we had our own rhythm. Coffee brewed in the octave of middle G. Same pot that formerly propped up my mother's good-bye note. I once asked Daddy why he'd kept it. The coffeepot. He told me, "No use throwing out a good appliance." Aunt Fannie said Daddy was a very practical man. *Humph!* Of course, I'd caught him staring at that coffeepot for hours right after my mother left. Like if he looked long enough, the note might reappear with an entirely different message.

Still, Aunt Fannie said *practical* meant "logical, orderly, and doing what needed doing when it needed to be done." And right now, one thing that needed doing was the dishes.

Dry the dish. Pass it along. Give it to Daddy. Grab another dish from the dishwasher.

Plates squeaked. Silverware pinged off china cups. F-sharp. *Ping! Ping! Ping!*

Dry. Pass. Whoosh. Plink.

Heat from the stackable washer-dryer filled the space around us. The air smelled of brewing coffee and lemon dishwashing soap. The dishwasher put some bass in the space. Bass clef keys, D and E. I called them belly grumblers because they were so deep.

Daddy cocked an eyebrow my way. "You playing music in your head again, Mouse?"

"Nope!" I snatched my fingers down. I had a habit of moving them in the air around me, tapping invisible keys.

He snapped his dish towel at me. "Quit telling tales," he rumbled. Definitely in the treble key of E. I giggled.

"Um, soooo..." I said. "Were you able to fix Miss

Clayton's guitar string?" I pretended I was focused on drying a cup. Daddy hiked up the same eyebrow.

"Why do I feel like I'm being set up?" he asked.

Dry. Pass. Whoosh. Plink. The rhythm played out in the treble clef notes, high with a ring to them. *G-A, G-A, G-A, G-A.*

"Um, because there is too little trust in the world?"

He grunted.

Miss Clayton was my teacher at Mountain View Academy of the Arts, a magnet school for K–8. I loved her class more than any class ever. She was the very best writing teacher in the whole entire world.

And she was single!

See, I had an idea.

Daddy had been hovering over me since my mother left. That meant practically four years of nonstop hovering. Much like everyone else in town, he worked extra hard to make sure that I didn't feel forgotten without a mother. He did a great job. He really did. Most of the time, anyway.

Lately, however, all his good-doing had begun to feel a lot like overdoing.

Like when I complained about feeling tired. Sometimes being around people all day at school made me feel like a cell phone that'd been off its charger too long. I told him so. *That couldn't be it,* he said. *The problem was probably psychological.*

That wasn't it?

Psychological?

Wasn't it bad enough my mother told me I "loooooooooved" sky gazing long before it was true; then Daddy told me I had "forgiven" my mother, even though I wasn't sure if that was true?

A girl your age needs to get out more and be with EVEN MORE PEOPLE to get EVEN MORE TIRED! That's what he told me. In the words of Faith, "*Ay, dios mio!*" *Oh, my God!*

I love my father. He meant well. But really, all his fussing? For goodness' sake! It wore me out!

But I didn't say anything. I was afraid to tell him that sometimes he made me feel about as damaged as the rest of the town did. Like when Miss Gladys, from down the block, took my face in her hands and cried, "You poor girl." Or the way the mailman was always asking, "Are you going to be all right?" I was afraid telling Daddy would make him sad like he'd gotten when my mother left.

My first idea was to run away, into the woods, and live among the wild deer. Then I thought about how hard it might be to keep my books from getting wet and gross AND trying to find decent paper to write my future novels.

Enter my new plan!

What if I helped Daddy find a lady friend?

He had not dated, not once, since my mother left. He was a good-looking guy, you know, as far as daddies go, and he was just *kinda* old—like thirty-six. He even had all his hair and teeth. Maybe if he had someone to spend time with, take to the movies, he wouldn't need to keep an eye on every single thing I did.

While we'd been cleaning, he told me to make sure to wear something warm when we left for breakfast. I mean, really! I knew how to dress myself. I was turning eleven in a month!

"I know how you operate, Miss Slick!" he was saying. *Dry. Pass. Whoosh. Plink. G-A, G-A...*

I said nothing.

He went on. "You broke the strings on your teacher's guitar on purpose," he said, putting away the last of the dishes.

My tiny laugh said, *Busted, sister!*

Still, I gave him my best "who, me?" look. He grunted again. Then he laughed, shaking his head. Of course I'd broken the strings on purpose.

Guitars, violins, violas, and mandolins covered several walls in our house. If anyone in the world could fix Miss Clayton's guitar string, it was Daddy. So as soon as she turned her back in class on Friday, I'd pried the strings loose and frayed one. Trust me, it had been a mercy killing. That thing was sorely in need of tuning. She didn't play the guitar; she just used it as a prop during our language arts class when we acted out plays.

"She's a nice lady, your teacher," he said, not looking at me. I turned away from him, nodding my head. Smiling like the Cheshire Cat in *Alice's Adventures in Wonderland*.

Next I had to dust all the furniture and instruments. As usual, I saved Cherie Amour for last. That was Daddy's fancy electric guitar that sat in the corner of the family room. Daddy used to be a most excellent guitar player, only he hadn't played Cherie Amour in a long time—not since my mother left us that note on the coffeepot. It was as if all the music went out of old Cherie Amour. Out of Daddy, too.

"Daddy, are you ever going to play Cherie Amour again?"

He blinked at first, like he didn't understand. Then he went into wicked air-band mode. He squeezed his eyes shut and made a face like he was jamming out on a super stage, guitar in hand. I jumped around and offered silent cheers and air-applause. He bowed.

"Thank you, thank you!" he said.

He was feeling silly this morning. Pretending to play his guitar. Feet wide apart. Tongue pushed out one corner of his mouth. Wiping fake sweat off his forehead.

I shook my head. *Oh, Daddy.* Sometimes I felt like the grown-up.

"Promise me one thing," I said with a sigh.

"What?"

"If you do play her again, promise you won't look like that while you're doing it!"

He wrinkled his brow. Made his deepest frown. Then leapt toward me. Made his eyes sort of bug out.

He growled. "You've awakened the monster," he said. "You've awakened Sea Bear!"

I gave him another head shake. Sea Bear. He started doing this thing when Junior and I were little kids. See, he used to work overnight shifts. At the sheriff's office. When he got home, he told us if we made a bunch of noise and woke him up, he'd turn into a mythical monster. A Sea Bear.

When we were little, it was funny. But I wasn't a dopey little kid anymore. Still, when I looked at him, he looked like he needed to be Sea Bear.

So I did my part. I pretend-squealed.

"No, Sea Bear! No!" I said, not sounding at all scared. Then he lunged at me, and I squealed for real.

He growled some more. Said, "Get up those stairs and get yourself into some clothes, brat. Or I'll be feasting on Mouse stew!"

"Aaahhhhh!" I half yelled, half giggled, racing up the stairs. I didn't stop until I reached the second-floor landing.

Below, I heard Sea Bear chuckle and walk away. I waited for a second. Let my heart rate chill out on its own. Then I took in the quiet of the second floor.

Listening, listening, hearing silence, hearing the house sigh and wood floors creak and groan. Hearing the gas furnace kick on with the metallic hiss of a dragon wearing braces. I used to think the furnace was a beast living in our basement. Used to be afraid that one night it would come alive and breathe fire over our feet. That was before I awoke to the note on the coffeepot. I've learned there are scarier things in this world than furnaces or basements.

I was listening for snores and snorts, like usual. Junior never went to breakfast with Daddy and me on Saturday mornings. Especially not during football season. Daddy was overprotective of him, too. He spent a lot of time bossing Junior around. Telling him, "Pull up your grades, boy. Stay out of trouble. Work on your technique." Daddy had a lot of advice and one main goal—to get Junior a full-ride football scholarship to Penn State University.

That was where Daddy had wanted to go. Almost made it, too. We heard that story a lot. If I wasn't hearing it at home, I was hearing it in the diner or at church or in the market or the small library tucked neatly into the edge of the woods. Always bumping into someone who knew Daddy when he was "Harrison Jolly's youngest boy."

How Daddy had played linebacker on the football team. Best in the state. His heart was set on going to Penn State.

Instead, he wound up marrying Junior's mama, Jackie Davis. After that, Daddy joined the air force. Later, he and Junior's mama split up, and after a while, they decided Daddy was better with Junior than she was. Daddy and Junior moved back to Harmony. He started fixing old instruments and playing bass guitar in the church as a hobby. Tinkering and instruments had always been his passion, he said.

Until he reconnected with his first love.

Chantel Marie McDonald. My mother.

Junior's room was dark. It reminded me of a sanctuary in Penn's Cave & Wildlife Park where animals laze around in caves scratching their butts. A smell like old socks, old cheese, and maybe a hint of something dead hid in the darkness.

"Junior?" I whispered, holding my nose. "Junior? Want to come have breakfast with us? I'm afraid I woke the Sea Bear. He might try to make Mouse stew." I half giggled.

So dark. Very cavelike. Except for the splash of bright gold sticking out of a pile of clothes on a chair. I reached out and tugged the thick fabric. It was the sleeve of a hoodie.

To my surprise, Junior rose onto his elbow. Instantly I could see his face, lit by a small rectangle of light from his phone. "Hands off my stuff, Cady Cat!"

His voice was part growl, part yawn. Had he just woken up? He was one of the few people who never called me that most hideous of hideous nicknames—Mouse—which followed me around everywhere. Church was the worst because a lot of the old people called me Little Miss Mouse. *Ugh!* Isn't that awful?

"Why're you awake?" I asked. I moved closer to the bed. Soon as I got near, he reached up, hooked an arm around my neck, and yanked me down. Not hard enough to hurt, just enough to annoy me.

"If you didn't think I'd be awake, why'd you bring your little butt in here?" he said, scrubbing his knuckles across the back of my head.

"Junior! Don't be such a donkey! Stop messing up my hair!" I yelled. I was laughing. Junior was ridiculous. And unlike Daddy and most people in town, he never treated me like I was broken. In fact, Daddy constantly yelled at him for playing so rough. I loved that he treated me like he would anybody else. He never acted like I was some poor little girl with no mother.

After shaking me around a little, he pushed his cell phone toward me. The rectangle of light shifted from his face to mine.

"Look," he said. I did. Pixels of light danced. He explained that at his school's pep assembly yesterday, he and a few of his big, strong guy friends dressed up like girls and sang a song from the seventies.

"Check this out!" he said.

Looking at the phone's screen, I saw three figures, psychedelic blurs of color, twisting and twirling while belting out an old-school tune, "Best of My Love," by this group called the Emotions. Junior could barely get the story out because he was cracking up laughing.

I said, "Oh, yeah. Sea Bear will really love that!"

He grunted. "That's why I used this app to make a filter," he said, practically doubling over with laughter from his own cleverness. "The filter changes how we look! Sea Bear might see the video, but he can't prove it's me!"

Wouldn't the whole point of doing something like this be to show how funny you are? Sometimes I just didn't get Junior and his high school friends.

"It is hard to tell it's really you," I said. "I mean, I hear your voices, but your faces? Everything's just weird looking."

He was still cracking up. "I know, right? I love it. Man, that's what makes it so funny. I'm putting it on my YouTube channel. Gonna get a thousand hits, I bet."

I shook my head. Being a high school boy must be perfectly tragic. Your feet smelled bad almost all the time. Your friends burped or made other bodily sounds at inappropriate times. Worst of all, you laughed at things—like singing with your friends while wearing dresses—that other people didn't think were at all funny. Poor Junior. He and his high school friends lived for funny videos on the Internet.

So tragic!

"Junior? You coming with us? To breakfast?"

He kept smiling at his creation. "Naw, Cady Cat. You and Sea Bear just go on. I'm gonna post this, then go back to sleep."

I left him grinning at his comic genius in the darkened, animal-smelling room. Most likely making gross body noises and scratching his butt.

♫ ♫ ♫

Twenty minutes later, Daddy and I were on Main Street, parking in front of the Big Orange Diner. I'd tried to get him to walk over from home. It was two whole blocks away. But, alas, Daddy was too worried I might catch cold or fall off a curb or contract Ebola. There wasn't even any snow on the ground, but there I was, wrapped up in so many layers of "protection" I felt like a burrito.

Downtown Harmony was spread over three long blocks that dead-ended into the mountainside. Post office, sheriff's office, hair salon, four restaurants and a Subway, a few vintage or secondhand stores. That was pretty much it.

Almost all of those businesses had at least one person working there who'd gone to Harmony High School with Daddy.

With my mother, too.

The Big Orange Diner had been part of the family since long before I was born.

When we got to the door, I drew a deep breath. Whenever I was about to be around a lot of people, I'd get this fuzzy, dizzy feeling, like I was having trouble breathing. I felt the same way when I went swimming at the Y with Zara. She thought she was a mermaid. I didn't enjoy swimming nearly as much. Being in the pool made me feel anxious, the same way I felt about being in crowds.

We pushed the door. The bell jingled. Noise from plates, cups, silverware, voices, and the jukebox rattled and roared in a bunch of different keys. It was like jazz music—brash horns blending with looping melodies.

When we stepped inside, the mood was friendly and conversations bumped into one another in a variety of pitches, octaves, and tempos. People glanced up from their meals. I grabbed Daddy's oversized hand, suddenly grateful for his protectiveness. A few diners waved at us. Most nodded and kept eating. Still, my heart raced, because I felt like every eye was staring at me. We found a booth against the wall.

Sofine, everybody's favorite waitress, sashayed over. Her uniform was navy blue. Her name was stenciled in white. Her skin was the color of dark-roast coffee, and her lipstick was lavender.

Oh, and her hair—a beehive style—was very, very old-school and TALL.

She flipped a cup out of thin air and started filling it. Her eyes fixed on me instantly.

"Good morning, Little Miss Mouse. Guess what I have for you today?" Her grin was broad and her voice rang of exaggerated manners and good cheer. Yet her eyes dared me to try to ignore her. Miss Sofine was one of those people who made it her mission in life to "help" me after my mother left. She always went out of her way to talk to me, and if I didn't make proper eye contact or sit up straight enough, she'd correct me. Because, of course, what I absolutely wanted more than anything was for yet another person to hover over me. Like Daddy wasn't enough of a hoverer on his own. I mean, really!

But it wasn't all bad. She loved finding books for me—new books, old ones, any book she thought someone my age might like to read.

Daddy said, "Sofine, hey there, girl." He used his BIG voice and grinned wide. In the diner, Daddy always made sure to sound like his usual loud, happy self. At least, the "usual" most folks in town remembered him for when he was growing up. Sometimes I watched his face and saw quick flashes of him concentrating, trying to make the happy more real.

Sofine, who had a BIG voice of her own, grinned right back as she passed a book to me.

"I've seen this book." I held it up. *The School Story*, by Andrew Clements. "I'll read it as soon as I finish reading this," I said, pulling out Sarah Weeks's *So B. It.*

"You're reading it again," she said. Her tone was dreamy as the Milky Way. Like rereading a book for the fun of it was absolutely the most darling thing in the world.

She asked if it was good. I told her I thought so.

Then she said, "I was down in Pittsburgh yesterday, went in a bookstore, and that's when I saw the book. I thought of you. You have to tell me what it's about after you read it."

After that she asked what flavor tea I wanted. I said mint. She grinned. Over the years I'd gotten used to people like Sofine behaving as if every little thing about me was heartbreakingly cute. My pixie haircut. My library books. My piano playing at church.

She managed to give me the same kind of expression people get when watching heartbreaking TV commercials about homeless dogs.

For goodness' sake, what girl could feel awesome when the whole town was looking at her like she was sadder than a basket full of abandoned puppies?

She must have noticed my expression. She said, "Now, don't you worry. Everybody'll be here for your birthday." I smiled, not feeling smiley at all. My hands felt itchy in my lap. I looked down.

Since my mother left, just about everybody Daddy knew—and trust me, that's a lot of everybodies—got together to throw me a big birthday party in the diner.

I hated it.

Daddy didn't even listen when, for my ninth birthday, I asked if it might be better if we just invited a few people out to dinner.

He asked why I didn't want to have it at the diner like always.

I froze. It wasn't like I had a speech prepared.

Later, I knew exactly what to say. That it felt beyond embarrassing for people to throw me this big sympathy bash. My life was turning into one of those documentaries on TV. People were treating me like I'd been kidnapped and on the news for months and months, and then the police found me living in a well with squirrels and a clever fox. Not cool.

Kids at school made fun of me. Okay, not exactly. But honestly, throwing a party for the poor girl whose mother skipped out? I wouldn't blame them if they did.

I wanted to tell Daddy that this year we should have dinner with Junior and maybe Zara and Faith. A few other friends and relatives like Miss Clayton and Aunt Fannie, too. Chinese was my new favorite. The daughter of the owner of Chin's, Mei-Mei, was in my class at school. She was the only person in fifth grade who was more quiet than me.

I realized Sofine was still at the table, looking me up and down. Her gaze lingered on my hair, and her face got that "aw shucks" expression. I groaned. She was going to baby-talk to my hair. Again. Please, not the baby talk.

She pursed her lips. She leaned close, as though my hair could hear her. She said, in a syrupy-sweet, baby voice, "Look at that cute little pixie hair. That's what they call it, right? Pixie? So cute!"

I wanted to shrink myself down really, really small. Climb into my water glass...and drown myself. Well, not drown. But hold my breath for a really long time until she went away.

Why did she baby-talk to my hair? Why would anyone, for that matter?

My mother always wore her hair short. Ever since I had enough hair to style, she kept mine clipped short, too. She said compared to other black women, we had really thin, wispy hair.

Even though my mother had been long gone and the

stylists at Faith's mother's salon asked every week if I was sure I wanted to keep cutting it, I kept it the same way. It was different than most girls' at my school. I liked that.

People like Sofine thought I was somehow trying to "be like" my mother. And so what if I was? Not everything about my mother had turned out wrong. I loved her hair, loved that that was something we had in common.

Sofine cupped my chin and turned my head back and forth. "You're so precious I could eat you up!" She said this almost every time I came in here.

I came in here a lot.

She meant well. But it had definitely gotten old. You know?

Daddy began talking loudly to two men from around town. The men around here always wanted to talk to him about football. And I never understood why grown men thought they needed to yell at one another when talking about football.

They were all, "ha-ha-ha" and "that Junior's gonna make a fine Nittany Lion next year" and "he's the best quarterback in the state right now" and more "ha-ha-ha!" In western Pennsylvania, the sun, the moon, and the stars revolved around the State College campus of Penn State University. Home of the Nittany Lions.

Daddy, wearing his blue-and-white Penn State cap, glanced at me and asked if I was all right, and of course I said yes because I did not wish to discuss my Not All Rightness in front of loud football talkers in the Big Orange Diner on Main Street.

"She's still quiet as a mouse, eh, Jeremiah? Hey, there, Miss Mouse!" The man waved at me. WAVED AT ME! Like I'd just appeared at the table. I wished I could jump up and do something totally dramatic and OUT-STANDING. But I just sat there mumbling.

Mouse! Why couldn't my mother have seen an adventure girl when she looked at me? Then maybe my nickname would be Pippi Longstocking-Songbird. Or Soprano Ninja. Anything except Mouse.

Now Daddy, the two footballers, and Sofine all started talking about me at once.

Did they not understand? I COULD HEAR THEM!

They were saying "oh, she'll grow out of her shyness"

and "be glad the cat's got her tongue now because my kid talks so much" and "blah, blah, blah, blah, *I don't even know what I'm saying I just like using my words*" and then more "blah-dee-blah-blah-blah."

Sofine looked at me with her head cocked sideways and said, "Look at her there in her nice choker and earrings."

My aunt Fannie told me every proper lady should have a "signature look." I didn't know what a signature had to do with how one looked. However, if Aunt Fannie believed a woman's style was important, I figured I needed a style of my own.

So I started wearing the matching set I got at Sam's Club—genuine real imitation pearls. I hoped they made me look sophisticated, like one day I would grow up to do BIG things.

Speak of the devil! Aunt Fannie bustled into the diner right then and uttered three magical words:

"I have news!"

3

Anytime You Need a Friend

Excitement rushed through the diner like wildfire. Aunt Fannie was like that. She didn't just show up. She made an *entrance*!

The scent of mountain air, crisp and cold like bright red apples, raced in ahead of her as she entered and did her dramatic twirl.

Once she was convinced that she had everyone's attention—and who could look away when she was wearing her Everyone-Pay-Attention red wool coat and matching red knee-high boots?—Aunt Fannie revealed that the pastor was naming a new choir director at the First Sunday Gospel Brunch the next day. We'd known it was coming, and everyone who went to the Church of Sunrise Blessings and Sweet Words of Joy, Hallelujah, had been waiting since Mr. Emmit died and Miss Betty decided to retire.

"And there's more!" Aunt Fannie announced with a flourish. Aunt Fannie did most everything with a flourish. It was quite spectacular to stand in line at the meat market with her. She even ordered sliced cold cuts with a flourish. I think it scared the butcher, even though he had very big knives.

Her voice dripped with drama.

No one spoke. Sofine stood perfectly still, the coffeepot raised. Daddy's cup hovered in front of his face. It was like freeze tag for grown-ups. Unlike me, Aunt Fannie loved being the center of attention.

"Tomorrow at the Lodge," she said, "after the Gospel Brunch, Pastor Shepherd will make the announcement."

She paused. Her eyes sparkled. In a voice dripping with her "you didn't hear it from me" tone, she whispered,

"I hear the new choir director is a man." *Gasp!* "And he's single!"

Several of the equally single women let out tiny gasps. You could practically smell the hairspray and lip gloss churning as they prepared their plans of attack. I was a little shocked that Aunt Fannie had said anything. I figured she might want to get first dibs. It just goes to show you that in Harmony, even the thought of snagging a single choir director ran a distant second to the thrill of sharing really good gossip.

♫ ♫ ♫

I lay on my back in Harmony Park, two blocks south of the diner. Stretched flat next to Zara, with fall leaves fanned out beneath us. We lay with our heads together but our feet pointing in opposite directions. Behind us, the mountain rolled upward. Peaks of green appeared to touch the sky.

Daddy was toward the edge of the wide-open lawn. Frowning. Probably worried I was going to come down with meningitis. Or measles. Or bird flu. Something. Anything. Yeah, he worried a lot. At least he wasn't embarrassing me.

Despite the chill of the morning, the afternoon was alive with sunshine, laughter, and the smell of smoke from nearby grills. Daddy and one of his friends were grilling hot dogs and burgers; chicken, too. I only ate the hot dogs.

Zara was saying, "...wish you could just go jump into a warm ocean?"

I turned my head so I could see her. "Nope! What if a shark bit me?"

She giggled. "Oh, silly. I'm a mermaid, remember? I'll protect you."

I shook my head and smiled. We both were silent for quite a while. Zara and I did this a lot when it was just the two of us. We could stare into the sky or color pictures for hours without talking much. We couldn't do that when Faith was with us. Faith was always moving, doing something. Today she was getting her hair braided, so it was like the old days. Just the two of us. Staring into the sky. Imagining worlds only we could imagine.

In Zara's world, she was a mythical sea creature with a magnificent tail. She was a protector and a conqueror and a beautiful defender of the sea.

My vision? It was so different. My vision was of the stars forming a map meant only for me. A constellation that would show my mother's face and how to reach her and tell her how I really felt. Tell her how much I wished Daddy and I could say good-bye to her and stop waiting for her to return. To ask her if that was okay.

Sometimes when the doorbell rang unexpectedly, for a brief second, I thought she'd be there. Waiting. And I never felt sure if the idea of her showing up made me happy or sad.

Zara's voice was soft when she finally spoke again. "Do you know where she is right now?"

I shook my head. Zara always knew what I was thinking. She took my hand and held it.

"Sometimes, at night when we'd look at the sky, she'd tell me about the Goddess Luna," I said, my voice practically a whisper.

"Goddess of the moon," Zara said.

Neither of us looked at the other. We lay perfectly still, smoky hot dog smells dancing in the air around us. A car radio off in the distance played. Whitney Houston, "I Will Always Love You." I flinched. The song was so faint, I wondered if I was the only one who could hear it. My whole body tensed. Zara squeezed my fingers, and finally I exhaled.

"She told me when I was a baby, she thought I was her moon goddess. As I got a little older and wouldn't talk to anyone, she started calling me Mouse."

Zara turned to look at me.

"You're much more of a moon goddess than a mouse," she said encouragingly.

I sighed. Then out of nowhere, a tune came into my head. A memory. As distant as the North Star. Had it taken light-years to reach me?

"*Blue Moon, you saw me standing alone*..." I softly sang. Automatically, my fingers hovered above my head, silently playing my invisible keyboard, my falsetto a whispery rendition of the higher scales, but *dolce*—very soft.

"What's that? Are we supposed to learn that for Mrs. Reddit's class?" Zara asked, still looking into the wide blue blanket of afternoon sky.

"No, it's a song my mother used to sing. You've heard that expression, 'once in a blue moon,' right?"

She nodded.

"A blue moon is what sky watchers call the second full moon in a month. My mother told me it meant something that was truly rare," I said.

I closed my eyes, just for a moment. Something hard and sharp poked me from the inside. My mother had sent me a cell phone for my ninth birthday. But her calls only came once in a blue moon. When she'd been here with me, I'd thought a blue moon was something magical and mysterious. I'd wanted to be a blue moon. Now I was afraid that was exactly what I'd turned out to be. Not mysterious, just so rare that I was odd. A freak. A blue moon in the heavens was cherished; here on Earth, I'd become the kind of rare that meant not being like everyone else. Not having a mother at home. Not having enough confidence to speak. A freak.

The next morning, the blue sky had turned watery. My jaws were clenched, and my fingers were gripping a large glass casserole dish filled with sweet banana pudding, and I was trying not to pass out.

Aunt Fannie was driving a hundred and fifty miles per hour. At least, that's how it felt.

Zoom! Zoom! Zoom!

Junior sat beside her in the passenger seat, his long legs bent awkwardly and his knees practically poking into his neck. He glanced over his shoulder, and his eyes were round like china saucers. When I tried to ask Aunt Fannie to slow down, she just laughed, cranking up the stereo in her bright blue little car that we called the Blueberry.

"Oh, honey, I'm barely above the speed limit," she said.

Her perfume mixed with hair spray, hair sheen, perfumed soap, and face powder to fill every inch of the tiny car.

"I don't think it's meant to go this fast, Aunt Fannie," Junior said. I tried not to laugh, but he sounded terrified. And that tickled me.

Aunt Fannie just sang louder, smiling like a maniac!

She had stopped by the house to pick us up as usual and to make sure I was dressed proper for church service. I liked how she fussed over my clothes and hair, making sure everything was just so. For all Daddy's futzing about, I tried not to let on how not having a woman around really made me feel. Without Aunt Fannie, Daddy would have had me wrapped up in Carhartt hunting clothes all the time. You know? For protection!

When she rounded another set of road curves, I clung to the seat belt, hoping not to go flying through the sunroof. If I let out a scream, would it be in a high C? I had hit that note before in front of Mrs. Reddit. Of course, afterward, I almost threw up.

I imagined holding the note so long that I burst all the windows in the Blueberry. The highest octave, in the key of A. Aunt Fannie probably would just tell me *bravo!* and drive faster.

She twisted in the seat and repeated the question she asked me once a week: "Honey child, I know how much you love your Mariah Carey. I'm singing one of her songs today, hallelujah! You sure you don't want to partner up with me? I'd be happy to have you."

"No, thank you, Auntie," I said. I knew she was just trying to be nice. She'd never heard me sing. Had no reason to believe I could sing. Even though she had been the one to make me a playlist of Mariah songs. Said she had picked them out personally because "some of her songs are more adult. But these are perfect for a little angel. Even one quiet as a mouse."

The Blueberry continued to zoom beneath a canopy of leaf colors in the early October morning. Aunt Fannie mashed the gas pedal and the car sped on.

♫ ♫ ♫

The Lodge was a huge restaurant tucked high in the hills. Twice a month, we held our Sunday services there. People could enjoy their brunches while the choirs performed onstage. Gospel Brunch drew folks from all over the state—sometimes even from out of state. Mostly, though, it was the same faces. Even the out-of-towners were familiar. Everybody was related to somebody and all the bodies were ready for music and a good breakfast.

No matter how scared I got about singing, I was always happy at the Lodge. Auntie said people who could sit there while the choirs performed "that good gospel music" and not feel it deep in their bones, well, their souls were truly dead.

I had to agree.

Speaking of death, I was so happy we'd made it onto the gravel parking lot alive that I practically stopped, dropped, and rolled across the ground.

Aunt Fannie completely ignored me as I said, "Thank you, sweet Lord Almighty!" She swooshed the banana pudding away from me and strutted toward the building.

I traded glances with Junior. It was natural for the church ladies to bring extra dishes for sale at Gospel Brunch, but we knew that wasn't why she was fanning that banana pudding around like some sort of red cape at a bullfight.

One quick glance around the parking lot told the story. Other women—single women—climbed from their cars holding heavy platters and plates. Offerings. Not for the public, but for the new choir director. That poor man was in for a lot of casseroles. And desserts.

When my mother left, Daddy used to get a lot of casseroles. Gradually, however, word spread that his heart was too beat-up for love. Every now and then, a woman would still approach him with a dish, but mostly just

Old Lady Moses. And that was all right, because she knew Daddy was crazy for her peach cobbler and her jerk chicken.

I wondered if Miss Clayton knew how to make peach cobbler. I'd have to ask her without saying why.

Before I even made it all the way up the front steps, still trying to figure out how to trick Miss Clayton into baking a cobbler, Faith and Zara came bursting through the double doors.

"Today is going to be awesome!" Zara said, hugging me tight. Faith, as usual, was doing some sort of complicated hand-clap, foot-stomp combination. The kind that cheerleaders do. Faith wanted to do anything that would make her stand out, almost as much as I wanted to do EVERYTHING not to stand out.

She grinned. "Hey, girl. The Husband Pageant has already begun!" Then she hand-clapped it out and topped it off with a "woo-hoo!"

Every time a new single man joined the church, all the single women broke out their best recipes, their best faux furs, and their absolute most expensive perfumes. We called it the Husband Pageant.

Who would be crowned the new Miss Missus?

Faith took a step forward and did a spin. It was all very elaborate and graceful. Perhaps on its way to becoming a flourish, even. Then she clutched her arms across her chest and thrust her head toward the heavens, her gazillion tiny black braids waterfalling over her shoulders. Her chocolate-brown complexion stood out nicely from the bright reds, pinks, and yellows of her scarf. After a long pause, she looked at Zara and me.

I tugged one of her braids and said, quietly, "Your hair looks nice."

She shook her head dramatically, making the long, thin braids dance.

"Girls! I can feel it," she said. "Something wonderful and amazing is going to happen today. You know how I feel about my girl Miss Grace Pendergast. I want to be discovered and become a singing sensation like her. And for some reason, I've got this crazy feeling like something is going to happen today!"

Then she collapsed into a curtsy and flung an arm across her eyes—to shield out the glare of all her potential, I guess. Zara and I were used to such displays from Faith. We were trying to help her get back on her feet when a blur of plaid whipped around us like a tornado.

"JONES!" we all yelled.

Abraham Jebediah Jones.

Faith wrinkled her nose. "Jones? What is that nasty smell on you?"

Everybody in the whole wide world called that boy Jones. Teachers included.

He was the size of a third grader. He wore plaid bow ties all the time. And thick glasses. AND he was about the most annoying creature on God's green Earth.

But you know what?

Here was the crazy thing—he sang like an ANGEL!

"Aw, baby girl," he said, pushing his face up close to Faith's, "you know you like my man smell!" Then he hit her with that dumb laugh of his.

Honk-honk-honk!

Really it was more like *Honk! Snort! Honk! Snort! Honk! Snort! Honk! Snort!*

Faith was still swinging at him when he vanished

down the steps and out of sight. A blur of plaid and boy smell. A well-behaved Jones was a once-in-a-blue-moon occurrence.

We headed inside. Unlike Faith, I was hoping there wouldn't be any surprises.

4

Someday

The next hour was a flurry of nervous activity—grown-ups rushing about, kids doing vocal exercises. The interlude between morning prayer service at seven AM and the later service featured the curly high notes of the classic church organ twiddling through gospel standards such as "Take My Hand, Precious Lord," and "Peace in the Valley."

When the ladies started making breakfast, the three of us bought pancakes and sausage with apple juice and found a table near the windows so we could see who was coming.

"Oh, my," said Faith, in her best Church Lady voice. Zara and I were already giggling. We loved to sit and watch people and make comments the same way some of the older women at the church did. Faith wrinkled her nose like one of the ladies we loved to imitate, and said, "Sister Loretta over there better be careful in those high heels."

Zara nodded, joining in. Making her voice as dry and nasal as she could, she said, "Heels so high, Sister Loretta must be trying to get closer to the Lord."

We tried holding it in, but laughter burst out around mouthfuls of pancake.

Right at that exact moment, the Trinity Sisters walked up. Not really sisters, but everyone called them that. I sharply inhaled. Held my breath. These women had become part of church legend.

The three of them paused in front of us. Miss Lily. Miss Wanda. Sister Dahlia. That was what they wanted to be called, and that was how they were addressed.

"Hello, ladies," said Faith, her tone wary. Zara and I jumped to our feet, clutching each other's hands. Fearful, but alert.

Miss Lily was the tallest. Like the other two, she wore

a colorful suit and hat large enough to launch into space. Her suit was yellow, to match the autumn leaves. She walked right up to me and placed her hands on either side of my face.

I blinked. Swallowed hard. Felt Zara take a step back.

Miss Lily said, "God has blessed you, child. You're an angel!" Her words started out soft, then grew more intense.

Miss Wanda fluttered her hands, saying, "Hallelujah!" then stepped over to us. She stuck her hand out and pressed her palm to my forehead, as if she were healing me. This seemed to please Sister Dahlia, who then joined her friends and placed both hands on my shoulders.

I shut my eyes, unable to even try to begin to understand what they were doing. Wait, what *were* they doing? I opened my eyes again and realized they were swaying ever so gently and singing words at such a low pitch it was impossible to understand beneath all of the noise in the hall.

When Miss Lily's eyes popped open, I jumped. Hadn't realized they were closed until now. She knelt so that I could look straight at her.

"We pray for you, sugar," she said.

"Amen," cried the other Trinity Sisters.

"No child should have to suffer what you have suffered," Miss Lily said.

"Suffered like a lamb!" said Miss Wanda.

"A mother leaving like that is a sin!" declared Miss Lily.

At that point I was a trembling mess. Zara and Faith had both taken two giant steps back, while several others passed by and threw glances in our direction like we were doing the hula with Eskimos.

Miss Lily shut her eyes tight and began, "God won't abandon you—you are a child of God, created by God, secured, accepted, and valued by God. You have direct access to God's throne of grace. Nothing can separate us from God's love. God will never abandon you."

The words of her prayer danced around my brain. *Abandon. Secured. Valued. Separate.* Words that conflicted with one another and made my heart squeeze. Daddy never spoke of my mother's absence as abandonment. He made it more about her needs. The Trinity Sisters had a different idea. The knot in my chest told me I might agree with them more than Daddy, a truth I did not want to think about.

Miss Wanda spoke in a dry, crinkly whisper. She said, "In the Bible, it says, 'I will fulfill my vows to the Lord in the presence of all His people.' Don't let your mama's absence make you lose sight of your responsibility to the good Lord."

"Amen!" cried the other two women. Then all three straightened. For the first time I realized their suits were exactly alike and each woman wore one color from head to toe. Miss Lily, as I'd noticed, in autumn yellow. Miss Wanda in deep cranberry. Sister Dahlia in frosty blue. Hat, scarves, suits, shoes.

They walked off, and Zara and Faith rushed back to my side. "Are you okay?" they asked.

Faith shook her head at me. "Girl, you just got Trinitied!"

I tried to laugh it off like everybody else, but Miss Wanda's whispery voice crackled in my ear like static from a radio far in the distance.

Will I fulfill my vows to the Lord in the presence of all His people?

It was as if I'd just gotten an e-mail from Heaven reminding me of my answered prayers. I had made a promise. Now the time had come to keep my end of it. I wondered if Miss Wanda was on God's e-mail list, too, and if she knew my secret.

Before long, we were getting ready to perform. The Lodge was filling up, and by the time we headed backstage, the parking lot beyond the tall windows was mostly full. Food smells swirled around, and the adult choir was already rocking and rolling while the deacons did their thing.

My knees were beginning to get jittery. The air backstage felt heavy. Despite having gotten Trini-tied for no good reason, what was really getting to me was seeing all the people. Feeling like they were looking at me. That trapped underwater feeling pressed against me, and I had to take deep breaths. Deep, deep breaths.

Just before time to go onstage, Faith whispered, "Oh, my goodness, Mouse! I can't wait to meet the new choir director. I just have this feeling—like everything is about to change." She held my hand and squeezed my fingers. We were inching along to our places in the shadowy area behind the stage. I struggled to catch my breath as my throat got tighter and tighter. I wished I felt as good about change as she did. To me, change always felt a little like an unexpected note on a coffeepot.

Besides, what if the new choir director was stricter than the others? Miss Betty, who'd worked with the Children's and Youth choirs since forever, knew me. She never pushed me to get off the back row and really sing.

Okay, so I knew I'd promised God I'd finally come out of my shell and sing like a bird and all, but what if I couldn't? Would the new choir director kick me out?

I will fulfill my vows to the Lord in the presence of all His people.

Zara took one glance at me and knew why I looked so nervous. She reached back and took hold of my hand. Her fingers were warm and strong. I could feel the comfort in the pulse of her veins and crook of her bones.

Sometimes when the two of us were out shopping or at the mall thirty miles away, people would see us, me and Zara, and ask if we were sisters. We both had skin that was somewhere between weak tea and apple-pie crust. Light, light brown. And we both had gray eyes. Although Zara had lots of green in hers; mine were mostly just gray.

Of course, the hair was totally different. While I wore my pixie cut, Zara had springy ringlets that reached all the way to her butt. More than once, I overheard women in Faith's mother's salon whispering about how Zara had so much hair because her father was white. Like that had anything to do with anything.

Anyway, I always felt like Zara and I didn't just look like sisters, we understood each other like sisters. Faith and I were close, but Zara was my best friend.

Before I could give it any more thought, one of the grown-ups backstage was pushing us forward and we were filing out onto the risers. Miss Betty directed us to our places. But when I got to my spot, she waved me over.

"Would you be so kind as to play for us this morning so that I may direct the children fully on my last day?"

Oh, good grief! I did not like surprises. I wanted to

say, *No, thank you very much!* But Miss Betty, with her old-lady glasses, smelled like peppermints and powdery perfume. She was one of the nicest people on the whole green planet. I simply nodded. At least I wouldn't have to suffer the brutality of singing background for our choir's resident diva, six-year-old Precious Henry.

I took a seat at the piano, adjusted the bench, and was about to begin when Miss Betty announced, "Because today is my final day directing the children, I will be accompanied on piano by the very talented Cadence Mariah Jolly."

For a second, I was certain I was going to pass out. Now, why'd she have to go and do that? Hot fiery needles of fear poked at my cheeks, and my hands began to shake. I reached for the music on the stand above me, but all I managed was to knock it to the floor.

When I bent over to pick it up, I almost fell. Light sounds of laughter floated from the risers.

Miss Betty came over and knelt gingerly to help. "You'll be fine, dear. You've played this music over and over since you were six. I have faith in you." My hands shook just a bit. *Deep breath. Deep breath. Deep breath.*

I didn't dare look out past the bright lights of the stage. Instead, I imagined I was inside a story. I saw myself dressed in ankle-length skirts and running around a large house as one of the girls in *Little Women* by Louisa May Alcott. Only, instead of being the headstrong, outspoken Jo, I could only picture myself as poor Beth. Helpless and pitied due to scarlet fever.

A little shiver ran through me, and I hoped I wasn't coming down with a real fever. I sat up straight, my gaze on Miss Betty. *Don't be Beth. Don't be Beth*, I repeated to myself. Then, following Miss Betty's lead, I began the opening notes to "This Little Light of Mine."

Precious Henry didn't so much sing as attack the lyrics, like she was belting some kind of fight song for a football team. Even so, people ate it up, right along with their bacon and waffles. She got tons of "go, girl" and "that's right, baby" and that sort of thing. Which seemed to make her sing even louder, though I wouldn't have thought it was possible.

And you know, by the end of it, I couldn't help thinking:

The idea of singing a solo audition is less terrifying than the thought of an eternity of singing behind the screaming antics of Little Miss Precious!

Mercifully, we had to witness only one screaming performance in the key of *YIKES!* courtesy of Little Precious. The Youth Choir was performing next. And Joya Booker and Terrance Walker had a duet.

"I love it when Joya and Terrance sing together," whispered Faith. We sat in chairs offstage as the Youth Choir took its place on the risers. Their purple robes and peaked white collars made them look like exotic birds. Joya wore her long hair pulled back into a grown-up-looking bun. People at church were always telling us girls we should look up to her. And we did.

As Joya took her place in front of the risers, she didn't seem particularly hurried or worried. Terrance came to stand beside her. His dark brown skin shone like buffed leather; his snow-white teeth blazed beneath the bright lights.

Miss Betty introduced them, but she didn't sit down to play. The Youth Gospel Band had taken the stage. Junior was up there looking all big-boy proud. His gray suit fit him perfectly. His mother, Miss Jackie, had the suit made special for him when he went to visit her in

Philadelphia over summer break. Miss Jackie called Junior all the time. Thinking about that tightened the knot in my stomach. Miss Jackie hadn't just left Junior with Daddy because she had something better to do. She'd pursued a career in the navy and thought her son would be better off living full-time with his father.

Maybe my mother figured I'd be better off full-time with Daddy, too.

Maybe.

The opening chords of the song began, and instinctively we all shifted forward in our seats.

"*Take me to the king*," sang Joya. Lyrics blossomed on her lips like springtime, growing brighter and more beautiful with each note.

Each breath seemed to define her name: Joya. Joyful. Joy.

Only after Faith reached over and touched my fingers did I realize I'd been playing my invisible piano. We smiled at each other, then continued to watch Joya. Faith leaned into me, whispering, "One day that's going to be me. Well, us. All of us. Right up there wearing those purple robes!"

The knot in my belly did a twist.

Terrance's rich tenor joined the light, sweet soprano of Joya's voice. The blend was pure melody. His voice, melding with hers, held a buttery quality. Their tones were rich, confident. My heart hammered in my chest.

What if God wanted me to sing? Oh, boy! Bad enough I'd made a promise to the Lord; was He making a request from me? I tried to imagine God's voice, what it would sound like. Asking me to use the gift He'd given me to sing. All I kept hearing in my head, though, was the pastor's voice.

Words to their song soaked into my skin, washed all through me. And when they were finished, I had tears in my eyes. Tears for the beauty of what they'd shared and how it had affected everyone in the building. Tears for the fear that even though Mrs. Reddit said I'd been blessed to sing, I may never find the nerve to show it.

Applause flooded the stage in waves after the Youth Choir finished. The preacher talked to the audience and prayed. Spending time at the Lodge was always like being somewhere between a church service and an inspirational TV show.

Soon enough, all the young people were ushered from

backstage and the adult choir members began to take their places. Somehow Faith, Zara, and I managed to elbow our way to a tiny area at the foot of the stage.

Anticipation, electric and sharp, pinged through the room. Diners set down their forks and cups. Everything else had been leading up to this. It was time for the Show.

Aunt Fannie stepped into a shallow pool of light. Like all the women in the adult choir, she was wearing her deep purple choir robe with the silky golden collar.

I felt a familiar flutter in my chest. Aunt Fannie may love attention, she was absolutely one of the worst drivers on the planet, and she was shameless when it came to tracking down single men in the church worthy, as she put it, of "evaluation."

But when she took the stage for Sunday Brunch, none of that mattered. She was poised and proper and beautiful and...and, whatever it was when you were just too good for people to look away. That was Aunt Fannie.

Behind her were rows and rows of her choirmates. A woman I didn't recognize was at the piano. The adult band combo was also onstage. Junior remained, looking like Daddy with his guitar poised at the ready.

The melody—Mariah Carey's "Anytime You Need a Friend," with a gospel arrangement—flowed from the band. Then Aunt Fannie began to sing.

Beside me, Faith sang along. She could not match the soaring heights of Aunt Fannie's notes, but her tone was raw and sounded pretty good. Zara's voice was higher, sweeter than Faith's, but she struggled with the high notes.

At that moment, I almost said it. I. CAN. SING. I wanted to be like one of the girls from my favorite books. Like Mo LoBeau in *Three Times Lucky*, who prays for the return of her upstream mother while she lives with people who love her but aren't her family. Or the girl in *So B. It*, Heidi, who can't stand not knowing her history and wants so desperately to understand her own story that she hops on a bus and runs off for answers.

Girls like that take action. Girls like me take cover.

It made me feel guilty, knowing my best friends had never, EVER heard me sing. Their voices may not have been perfect, but I felt their sincerity, their happiness, through their whispered attempts to match Aunt Fannie note for note.

What was wrong with me? Why did I have to be such a . . . *mouse*?

In my mind, I saw it plain as day. Saw myself getting swept up in the song's lyrics, blessed by their meaning. Saw myself turning to Zara, then Faith, and admitting that I'd been keeping this HUGE secret because I had been afraid. Inside my head, as Auntie's voice rang out clear as a church bell, moving notes around as though each was written just for her, I tried to picture us up there together. Then I got a pang from someplace deep inside. *Not me and Auntie.* I really wanted to sing a duet with my mother. If only my mother could be here. How perfect would that be? Me joining her onstage, sharing my blessing with everyone AND keeping my promise. Somehow I knew if my mother were to come back, even for one day, I'd find the courage. I would. I really would.

Faith slung an arm around my shoulder. Even though I'd never told her about my voice, and in all our years of being in choir together where she'd never heard me flat-out sing, she knew about my fantasy. About how I didn't want to think badly about my mother for leaving. How I wished her well and much happiness because, after all, that was what Daddy told me to do. But how I still hoped.

Out of nowhere, a rush of tears welled in my eyes.

"Excuse me," I said, before taking off toward the back of the hall.

Standing in the semidarkness behind a wall of people, I humphed and huffed, blowing air through my cheeks and nose, not at all sophisticated.

My heart did its caged dance in my chest. I shut my eyes and felt myself absorb each note. Salty tears leaked quietly down my face. I swiped them away, one by one. And without even realizing it, I began singing, too. My voice curving around, blending perfectly with Aunt Fannie's.

If only I'd had the courage to stand on that stage and let myself go the way Aunt Fannie did.

My hand went gently to my chest, a light falsetto trailing my notes as Auntie climbed higher and higher. I was matching her tone and sound with an ease that surprised me, even though I was not singing full out. Mrs. Reddit told me it is not about who can sing higher, but who can control their notes as they move higher and lower.

Lightly, I touched my throat. Felt the pulse of my vocal cords as my voice whispered through the musical registers.

Then I felt a presence.

A plaid bow tie to my right.

Jones.

And he was looking at me with the most curious expression.

Had he heard me?

Funny thing. The idea of Jones hearing me at that moment didn't terrify me. Not one little bit. Still, I scurried away before he could ask any questions.

Have you ever felt like you couldn't decide whether you were terrified or thrilled?

That was how I felt after our pastor thanked Miss Betty for her service, then introduced the new director and his assistant.

Miss Clayton had joined us. Faith and I exchanged looks. I had told her and Zara about my plan to get Miss Clayton and Daddy together. We smiled extra sweetly at our teacher, and she knelt and gave my shoulder a squeeze.

"What do you think, Cadence? He looks like a nice man. Maybe he'll be a wonderful new addition to the church," she said, staring up at the new director. Then a few of the old ladies beneath church hats as wide as helicopters called out, "God is good!"

Which drew the usual response of "Every day! *Amen!*"

From where I stood, I got a good look at the new choir director. Mr. Bassie was a tall man who reminded me of a real-life Easter Bunny. With skin a rich chocolate brown and sort of a barrel shape going on, all he needed were big feet and fuzzy ears. But his smile was dazzling, his pants pleats were creased sharp as knives, and the polish on his patent-leather shoes sparkled beneath the stage lights. He was very outgoing, asking, "How's everybody doing this morning?" As soon as he sat at the piano, he began to play, talking all the while. He was really good, and after a time I forgot to be excited or thrilled or terrified. Like everyone else, I was just enjoying the whole show.

Then, as he played his medley, he began to tell us how he grew up in Pittsburgh and had a rough life. How he fought against negative influences trying to stop him. How he stumbled along the way, but soon as he discovered his love of music, he knew "the Lord had made a way for me. He showed me a path, but it was up to me to take the first step. I have been high-stepping ever since. Amen."

"Amen!" answered the audience.

I got a shiver when he said that last part because, I knew it was weird, but it seemed like he was looking right at me. Like he knew I was going through a rough time and had something to overcome. Like he knew I wasn't fighting for what I wanted the way I should.

But, really, did I even know what I wanted?

I'd promised God and myself and my friends that I'd try out for the Youth Choir and sing better and all that, but was it what *I* wanted?

That was when Zara slid over next to me, saying what a nice man Mr. Bassie seemed to be and didn't I think I'd be able to go through with my audition? When Miss Clayton made a face like she didn't understand, Faith explained, "Me and Zara turned eleven last month. Mouse turns eleven next month. We're all pretty desperate to get out of the kiddie choir and into the Youth Choir. But with Miss Betty, you have to audition in front of everybody to move up."

Miss Clayton said, "And, Cadence, you feel like your shyness is holding you back?"

I nodded. Next thing we knew, Mr. Bassie was making a few big announcements of his own. First, he introduced us to his young assistant, a woman called Miss Stravinski. He said she'd work primarily with the Youth and Children's Choirs. Zara was thrilled. She grabbed me and told me I couldn't be scared of this choir director's assistant because she looked so young, like she was practically our age. I supposed that Zara was unable to see me turning green with terror right at that very moment.

My mind must have wandered off someplace because, the next thing I knew, Faith was giving me a hard shove with her shoulder. She was saying, "Oh, my goodness!" and other people were gasping. Oooohing and ahhhhhhing all over the place. I was lost.

What?

What?

What?

Onstage, Mr. Bassie was grinning. He had left the piano bench and was standing near the front of the stage, nodding his head.

He said, "We have a little less than six weeks to get ready for the big Gospel Music Jamboree the day after Thanksgiving. I knew when I accepted this position that I wanted to get to know all of my singers, but especially my young people. I know what music did for my life growing up, and I want to make it the best possible experience for all of you. That's why I am opening up the recording studios at the church to all you beautiful young people. And I am encouraging you, in the spirit of fellowship and community, to work as duos, trios, or quartets. Form singing groups among yourselves and record videos using the equipment at the church. You must each introduce yourselves and tell me a few things about you. That way, not only do I get to evaluate your voices, I get to know a little bit about you, too. Miss Stravinski and I will go through the videos separately. For those young people in the Children's Choir who are of age, the video can serve as your audition, and for all students, the videos will be used to assess your skill level. Oh, I almost forgot the best part. The performances that we like most will earn spots as highlighted performers at the Gospel Jamboree!"

A thousand pinpricks of electricity charged through

me. Highlight performances at the Jamboree were a big deal. Zara and Faith looked so happy. Miss Clayton smiled, but her eyes showed concern, like she knew exactly what I was feeling.

I couldn't help wondering... if my mother were here, would her face show the same concern?

"We're going to be the best young trio ever!" said Faith. One look at her, and you could see the ideas flooding into her head.

The room was in an uproar. Mr. Bassie went back to playing piano. The whole band played with him, so it got loud near the stage. We moved back toward the entry, where there were fewer people. Faith was pacing. She got like that when ideas started filling her head.

It was just the three of us. Faith walking back and forth, Zara twirling like a mermaid caught in a waterfall—and me, standing rigid, like my feet were made of ice.

It's Like That

Sunday, after church, Daddy told Junior and me that he was going out for a while. "You got a date, old man?" Junior asked, grinning. If I hadn't seen it with my very own eyes, I wouldn't have believed it: My big, strong, overprotective father actually blushed.

He scowled at Junior, looking at him from head to toe. Junior had dressed to go running. When Daddy looked at me, he saw that I had, as well. Lyra was hopping around on her leash, bark-bark-barking at the air. Daddy seemed to notice all of this for the first time.

"I don't want her catching cold," Daddy said, nodding in my direction *and* cleverly changing the subject. Naturally, when I tried to cut in and say I'd be fine, he and Junior started arguing about how cold it was or was not, and Junior was all "she'll be fine" and Daddy was all "it's chillier than you think," and Junior rolled his eyes and then Daddy rolled his eyes.

Now, if I were truly a drama queen, I would have stomped my foot or gotten all huffy. I mean, *really*! But instead, I inhaled and gave a little wave.

I said, "Excuse me, I'm right here. We're not going far, Daddy." Then, because I was a Future Bestselling Author with Amazing Powers of Observation, I looked at Daddy in his nice long wool coat and perfectly clean black leather gloves.

I asked, "Daddy, do you really have a date tonight? Is it with Miss Clayton?" My hands were enveloped in soft raspberry-colored gloves, so when I clapped it didn't really make a sound. Once again, his clay-colored cheeks darkened to a deep cranberry. Can't you just picture that! So sweet. Anyway, he finally cleared his throat and answered.

"Yes, well, um, this afternoon. An early supper. Maybe a movie, too," he said, looking guilty.

I let out a big, happy sigh.

But he bent down until we were eye to eye. "Are you really all right with this, Mouse? I'm just getting to know her. It's nice to have another grown-up, a lady, to talk to," he said. Then he paused, looking flustered. Finally, he went on, "You know, you'll always be my Number One girl."

I smiled. "Daddy, it's perfectly fine. Miss Clayton is awesome. Have a good time."

Junior piped in, "Yeah, old man. Just don't take her dancing. I've seen your moves. Trust me, seeing you dance would definitely kill the romance!"

Daddy and Junior exchanged some fake boxing jabs. I wondered if all men preferred to throw punches at each other rather than hugs.

"...shouldn't be worrying about my love life," Daddy was saying. "All you need to focus on is those colleges. And the only one that matters, Penn State!"

Junior backed away, shaking his head. "Is that right, old man?" Junior was smiling, at least his lips were, but his eyes...his eyes seemed to be focused far away.

"Boy, I'm going to get you into that football program if it's the last thing I do!" Daddy said.

With that, Daddy threw one more jab at Junior and headed out. Junior dodged, swatted Daddy's hand, then angled me and Lyra toward the door.

I liked running with Junior. He listened to music when we ran, but he only wore one side of the headphones. You know? For safety.

I liked the quiet. The way you could feel like it was only you and your heartbeat. I shut out almost everything. Pretended I was in a world of my own.

The new choir director's introduction and his announcement about the videos kept replaying through my mind.

What was I going to do? I didn't know if I was ready to record myself singing. Not with Faith and Zara standing there looking at me.

Or was I?

Junior stuck out his arm, blocking my path. We were at an intersection, and a big truck was rumbling past. Lyra barked excitedly. The truck passed, and Junior steered us toward a side street.

I thought about it. I had to figure out a way to tell

Zara and Faith about my secret. It was crazy to think that I'd been singing more and more when I was alone, that I fantasized about singing in front of audiences, but that I didn't have the courage to tell my best friends.

Junior continued running. I stared up at him. His eyes looked squinty, like something was bothering him. He was the most popular kid at Harmony High and one of the best athletes in the state. So what was on his mind? He glanced down at me and gave a quick smile.

Even if he was a half brother, Junior had always felt 100 percent to me. I was sure that nothing could be troubling my big brother. Me, on the other hand, I was plagued with troubles. Plagued.

Really, what was I going to do?

♫ ♫ ♫

Monday at school, I was so excited to see Miss Clayton. I waved at her, but tried not to stare so she wouldn't know I was wondering about her date with my dad. While the other students were settling in, I took out my personal journal.

Flipping the pages, I found the spot where I'd started writing last night—the spot where I'd begun working on a story about a girl like me, with friends like Faith and Zara, and a secret she needed to share.

While Miss Clayton called the class to order and asked how our weekends were, I sat hunched over the journal, tapping it with my pencil.

* What if I made my main character, the girl like me, have special powers?
* What if she had some kind of magic potion that made her feel like she could do anything and she just told her friends about her secret?
* What if she wrote them a letter?

I was stopped from going further, however, when Miss Clayton came over and touched my hair. “I can see someone is eager to begin lessons this morning,” she said, standing at my side. Several kids groaned, and I knew they were thinking I was even more lame and uncool for writing in my journal without being asked.

I stuffed my pencil and journal away, although she assured me I’d have plenty of time for that later. My cheeks felt hot from the stares of my classmates. When I peeked around, I didn't see anyone looking at me—I just knew that they had. I just knew.

We started our lessons and went to work like normal. I couldn't wait until it was writing time. I wanted to work on one of my stories. Only, when the time came, Miss Clayton made an announcement that almost broke my poor little heart in two.

Noooooooooooooooooooooooo!

Oh, Miss Clayton! How could you?

I felt myself start to tumble inside.

Here is what she said:

"Students, today we are going to shake things up a bit. Based on some test results from several weeks back, we're offering our highest-scoring students an opportunity to work with Mrs. Reddit, while the other fifth-grade teachers and I will work with the rest of you. Believe me, for those of you chosen, it's a great opportunity. And for everybody else, we'll have fun, too!"

There I was, preparing for the best part of my day. And then this.

My hands started to shake. On the board, there were only three names—mine, Mei-Mei's, and Sophie Cohen's.

Miss Clayton glanced at me with a hopeful look, but the only look I could make on my face was one that said, *Doom! Doom! Doom!*

"I thought you'd be pleased," Miss Clayton said as I stumbled over my own feet heading for the door.

"But I want to stay with you," I whispered. My voice sounded very small.

She gave me her understanding smile, but I wasn't sure she understood at all. This was not what I had expected. I was *really* not a big fan of surprises.

I followed Mei-Mei and Sophie out the door.

♫ ♫ ♫

Earlier, all anyone had wanted to talk about was Mr. Bassie and the upcoming Gospel Jamboree. Now ten of us sat in Mrs. Reddit's music room, not talking about anything. Even Jones was quiet, which was almost as shocking as him being among the highest-scoring students on the pretests we'd taken back in September. Everybody in here had done a good job, Mrs. Reddit told us. Still, it felt like being punished for doing well. I mean, *honestly*!

"I'm so happy to have you, students," said Mrs. Reddit.

She was a tall woman. Her skirts were long and straight like black pencil cases. Her tights were always black. Her hair, also black, always sat in a knot on the top of her head. Gold-rimmed glasses winked in the fluorescent lights, sparkling against her skin.

She explained that even though she'd been teaching music almost her whole life, she had another love, too. Literature. Specifically, poetry.

"I minored in literature in college and spent some time doing music therapy with children, incorporating storytelling and poetry," she added.

Everyone looked at her dully. I was sure they wondered what that had to do with us. I wrapped my arms around my body, trying to stop the shaking that crept into my bones whenever something new happened.

She continued, telling us how the fifth-grade teachers wanted to expose their top students to poetry.

"I love poetry and how it uses language," she said. "I hope over the next several weeks, I can teach you to love it, too."

I sighed, deeply and maybe more loudly than I'd expected. I didn't want to learn poetry. I wanted to write stories. I wondered if this was how Alice felt when she tumbled down the rabbit hole into Wonderland. Mrs. Reddit was starting to sound like the Mad Hatter!

Not until Jones placed a hand on my arm and asked, "Are you all right, Mouse?" did I realize how badly I'd begun to shake.

Razor-sharp pinpricks seemed to poke my face. I bit my lips, turning my mouth into a flat line, signaling I did not want to speak. Jones moved his hand away, but edged his seat close to me. I guess that made me feel better.

Mrs. Reddit passed out copies of a poem. "Suspense," by Pat Mora. We sat at a square table with hard chairs, away from the rows of instruments and the risers where we stood for choir, and the various instruments and sheets of music poking out of cubbies along the walls.

She asked us to read the poem to ourselves and prepare to discuss it.

My face felt hot, but my insides felt ice cold. I did not want to discuss anything. I did not want to talk. Out loud. In a group. No, thank you very much!

I read silently:

Suspense

by Pat Mora

Wind chases itself

around our house, flattens

wild grasses

with one hot breath.

Clouds boil purple

and gray, roll

and roil. Scorpions

dart

under stones. Rabbit eyes peer

from the shelter of mesquite.

Thorny silence.

My paisano, *the road runner*

paces, dashes into the rumble,

race from the plink, plink

splatter into his shadow, *leaps*

at the crash *flash*

splash,

sky rivers rushing into arroyos and

thirsty roots of prickly pears,

greening cactus.

The words rushed across the paper, forming their own meaning in mismatched lines, no rhyming and too many images to see at once. What I had always disliked about poetry was how sometimes you could read it but not have a clue what it was talking about.

Now Mrs. Reddit came over. Her face was expectant. She dropped into a chair next to mine.

"What do you think?" she asked.

No one spoke.

The big hand on the clock ticked.

Then it tocked.

But no one spoke.

And then...

"I liked it!" said Jones.

Groan. Groan. Groan.

I was hoping everyone had hated it. If everyone hated it, maybe she would let us go back to writing narratives.

She grinned at him. "What did you like about it, Mr. Jones?" she asked.

He sort of hunched his shoulders up and down. "I don't know," he said. "I guess just the way the words felt like what he, the author dude, was saying."

When Jones called the poet "the author dude," several kids chuckled, especially once Mrs. Reddit pointed out that Pat Mora was a woman.

Then she told us the technique of using words that sound like what they describe is called onomatopoeia. My mind slid the word around, liking the way it felt. I tried it out in my head—on-o-ma-to-poeia. *Onomatopoeia onomatopoeia onomatopoeia...*

Then I felt something else—panic. In Miss Clayton's class, there were twenty-seven students. No time to focus on the one or two quiet kids not making trouble. Too many kids all too familiar with trouble, competing for a chance to win an all-expenses-paid trip to the principal's office.

Not so in Mrs. Reddit's class.

She eyed us, one by one. Her gaze paused on me.

"Cadence? What did you think?"

Everyone looked at me. The hot pinpricks returned to my cheeks, only now they felt electric. Jabbing. Jabbing. Jabbing.

My throat felt tight and dry.

I hated surprises. I hated change.

Why couldn't things just go back to the way they were?

Jones poked me in the ribs with his bony elbow. "Aw, she liked it, Mrs. Reddit. Didn't you, Mouse? C'mon. Didn't you?" He was jabbing me, waggling his eyebrows up and down. He wanted me to laugh. The others around us looked amused, like they wanted to laugh, too.

I even wanted to laugh.

But I couldn't.

It felt embarrassing and overwhelming, being put on the spot like that.

Disappointment washed over Jones's hopeful expression. Even his ridiculous bow tie seemed to sag. I turned away, not wanting to see his eyes.

Mrs. Reddit smiled and said, "Don't worry, Cadence. We're a small group, and I want everyone to feel comfortable." When I glanced up, our eyes met. For a second, I thought I saw disappointment there, too. My insides sank even lower.

Then she moved the keyboard over to the semicircle. "Grab the bench," she told me. I did.

"I tell you what," she said. "Cadence, I want Jones to read the poem. You listen to his pace, find your key, and match his tempo."

I drew a deep breath, chewing my lips and not looking at anyone. Well, of course, Jones wasn't afraid of anything. He jumped up, holding the poem. He glanced over at me. Cleared his throat. I rolled my eyes.

Jones began slowly. I moved my fingers across the keys. Then he went a little faster and a little faster.

Anyway, Jones was reading away, and I was playing away, and when we got to the end, my inner Aunt Fannie must have taken over because I whipped my hand along several notes in a glissando, which on a piano is how to end a song in a flourish!

The class applauded, and Jones took a deep bow. Some of the fear melted off me. My heart pounded with relief. I'd felt the rhythm on the inside. And I smiled.

"Thank you, Mr. Jones, and you, too, Miss Jolly," Mrs. Reddit said.

We talked some more about the poem, then Mrs. Reddit gave us an assignment.

"Look for the personifications in the poem. Does

anyone know what *personification* means? It's when we give objects or other nonhuman things human traits."

I instantly loved the word. Per-son-if-i-ca-tion. And I'd loved *onomatopoeia*, too.

Was it possible that I was going to enjoy Mrs. Reddit's class after all?

Make It Happen

Never in the history of the Gospel Music Jamboree had a Youth or Children's Choir performance been FEATURED—except for Joya and Terrance, and they're amazing. Being featured was usually for the grown-up choirs. It meant getting your name in the program. Being treated like a star. Not that I expected or even wanted it to be us. Because, believe me, I did not. Really, I didn't.

Okay, maybe I did wonder about it—but just a little!

Mostly, the idea of being the center of attention like

that scared the sweet holy Mariah out of me. However, Faith had been barely able to sit still at school. For her, us getting chosen would be a dream come true.

We decided to go to my house after school to practice. My nerves had been stomping around my stomach all day. All this time they'd been convinced I couldn't sing. What would they do when they figured out I could sing, but was just too much of a mouse to do it?

A huge braided rug covered the wood floor in my room. Faith stretched out on her tummy, busy searching the Internet for the perfect song. Zara came into the room, twirling and swirling.

The way she twirled around made her look like a real mermaid. Light reflected off my walls, painting her in a watery glow. Daddy had painted them a cheerful blue. Never mind that my favorite colors were pink and red. One day a few years ago, I came home from school, and—voilà!—Daddy had painted it blue. He said he read in a book about parenting that blue was a calming color. Said blue would make me feel more secure than pink. Since my mother left, Daddy has read A LOT of parenting books. *Sigh!* He works so hard to fix me.

I sat propped against a huge pillow, my legs stretching out, rereading the poem from Mrs. Reddit's class. After, like, fifty times, I had to admit, there was something about it.

The way the words

moved. The way they looked

on the page.

Regular story writing didn't look like that.

Still, just knowing I'd have to leave my regular class every day made me feel dizzy inside.

So when Faith cried, "I've got it! I know what song we're going to record for Mr. Bassie!" it took a minute for me to understand. I felt like I'd been trying to breathe underwater.

Faith jumped up on her knees, holding her tablet out in front of her. Zara, who'd been lying on my bed, and I crowded in. Faith showed us a music video with two female singers. The women were quite smiley. The song they were singing was up-tempo. A make-you-wanna-get-up kind of song.

"It's Mary Mary!" said Zara with a shriek. Zara loved all kinds of music. However, I happened to know that the gospel singers who called themselves Mary Mary (by the way, both had names that were not Mary...) were her absolute favorites.

"'In the Morning' would be perfect for us to sing," said Faith, talking about the song in the video. "Even though it's one of their older songs, it's fast and easy to learn, because we've been singing it along with the radio for years. And it's the kind of song that just makes people feel good."

I chewed on my lip. When I saw they were both looking at me, I chewed harder.

"You can do it, Mouse!" urged Zara.

Faith tossed her waterfall of jet-black braids. She dropped her tablet onto my bed and stood.

"You can do it! Yeah. You're gonna do it, yeah! *C-A-D*"—*clap, clap*—"*E-N*"—*clap, clap*—"*C-E*"—*clap, clap*. She cheered. "She's gonna do it, do it, do it, is gonna do it, YEAH!" Then she did a kick and a cartwheel.

Well, I don't know about you, but if someone does a cheer with your name in it, you feel sort of obligated to live up to it. *I wonder if Junior and the rest of the football team feel like that, too? Hmm...*

Then the door opened and Aunt Fannie stepped into my room.

"Girls? Everything all right in here? I can barely hear anything down on the first floor," she said, looking around.

Daddy insisted that Aunt Fannie come by and "sit with" me after school, even though I'd told him a million times that I didn't need her to. I had to admit, though, having Aunt Fannie in the house made me feel better.

She came over and placed an arm around me. Today she wore a royal blue skirt that hugged her round hips. Her blouse was hot pink, and her makeup was movie-star quality. She said, "Sugar, how do you feel about all that's happening with the choir? Are you ready for so much change?" And before I could answer, she added, "And I think your daddy is sweet on that teacher of yours."

Aunt Fannie was carrying a tray with sandwiches, fruit, and sweet tea. She had lived in Mississippi for a long time. She served sweet tea with just about everything.

Faith grinned. "Don't worry, Miss Fannie. We're

helping our little Mouse." When she said the "our little Mouse" part, her voice got scrunched like baby talk. It reminded me of Miss Sofine at the diner baby-talking to my hair. *Sigh!*

The fiery needles poked at me, so I started counting backwards from a hundred. In my mind. Where no one could hear.

"I'm fine, Aunt Fannie," I mumbled.

The worst lie ever. Lyra, who'd been sleeping in the corner, rose up and eyed me, and I swear she shook her head in pure agony for my too-shy ways.

"Well, you know I love you, sugar. Anytime you need me, come see your old auntie," she said. She closed the door, and Faith retook center stage.

"Fannie is so nice," Zara said. "You're so lucky to have such a great aunt."

I couldn't stop the next thought that popped into my head. Why couldn't my mom be here being nice? I knew Zara was right about Aunt Fannie, but the questions tugged at my heart.

Would I be better off if my mother were here?

Would she be able to love me if she came home?

Or did I even want her to come back at all?

Turning to Faith, I could see she was all about the goal: getting a place in the spotlight at the Jamboree. She definitely wanted to get FEATURED!

She set about putting us in our places. "We have to think about my girl Grace Pendergast," she said. "She is amazing and just got a record deal, thanks to her videos online. If we can get good like her, I know someone will see us and want to give me a record deal."

"Me." Not "us." Zara and I exchanged glances but said nothing. Once we were settled into position, we tried singing the song through a few times. It didn't sound great. Definitely not Grace Pendergast worthy.

For one thing, I was sure Faith had underestimated the song's speed. Playing the keyboard and piano, not to mention a few other instruments, one thing I'd learned was that songs might sound simple, but sometimes those were the hardest to play.

Singing was that way, too.

It was one thing to sing along with Mary Mary. It was another thing to sing along and keep pace.

And sound good.

And not get winded.

Okay, I knew I might not be singing at my best because I was still scared to Pluto and back, but still... I mean, it was hard to sing well when your face was a raging, red-ant fire of embarrassment and fear.

RAGING FIRE.

So I accepted my responsibility. However, Faith didn't hit all the notes the way God or Mary Mary intended. The sisters made the song seem effortless and fun. Trying to match them, however, left us sounding like we were running in the rain. Not to point fingers, but it left one of us more winded than the others. (Not me. Not Zara.)

After fifteen minutes of frustration, Faith came up with an annoying observation, but a pretty good idea:

"We don't sound as good as we could. Probably because of you, Mouse. You can't be fake singing. You've gotta do better. So, I've got an idea," she said.

She said we should all put in our headphones and practice singing with Mary Mary to get comfortable. After fifteen minutes or so of practice, we could try singing together without them.

I swallowed hard. Took a long sip of iced tea. Popped an apple slice into my mouth. When I looked at Zara, her expression was gentle and encouraging. She smiled and nodded at me. Faith narrowed her eyes.

"You can do this, Mouse!" she said.

We spread out, earbuds in place. I went to a spot that was as far away from the other two as I could get. I lay on my back and closed my eyes. I let the song move through me, from my head to my toes. Listened with all my heart and felt myself lifted into the story the singers were describing in snappy, dancey verses.

My heart was banging its snare drum rhythm again. I felt absolutely positive my tongue would fall out. I gulped down the remaining sweet tea. Followed that with another glass, trying hard not to look at my two friends as I tiptoed across the room to the pitcher, then back to my little spot away from them.

However, after a few tries, it got easier. And easier. I pictured myself in the video with Mary Mary. The first singer starts out telling a story. She's telling someone who is having a hard time, "*When it's dark in your life, just wait for the daylight.*" The background is darkened, yet tiny dots of light, like fireflies, are shining, showing the promise of better times.

At first, I felt myself whisper-singing, a tight falsetto tickling the back of my throat. I cranked up the volume on my tablet and shut my eyes tighter. Shut out everything. Well, almost everything. Lyra plopped down beside me. I could feel her tail wag against my leg. Still, I concentrated on the words until I felt myself in my own video.

The words painted a picture in my mind. Faith, Zara, and me, moving through a beautiful green space. Our faces are turned upward toward the sky. We are beaming like rays of sunlight. We are shining on someone who needs us—needs our song....

I was not aware of exactly when it happened. When I lost myself inside the song and began to sing. Really sing. But I did. My hands were stretched out above my head. I made a fist that pumped to the eighth notes. I felt the rhythmic changes in tempo shift inside me like a pulse. When I needed to climb the musical scale, I touched my hand to my heart, the same way Aunt Fannie did, and opened my mouth to push out all the air and song in my body.

When I finished, I felt the warmth of the smile on my face. Felt the rush of adrenaline in my heart and fingers and toes. It was a beautiful feeling.

Then I opened my eyes.

And found Zara and Faith standing over me. Not wearing their headphones. Both staring, mouths open.

After keeping my secret for so long, I had finally shared it with my friends.

"What?" I squeaked. My body went into high alert. *WARNING! WARNING! Red Fire Ants of Shame heading your way!* Boy, did that snare drum in my chest go crazy.

"Moon Goddess?" Zara said. Ever since I'd told her the story about how I wished my mother had kept calling me that, Zara had started herself. So far, it hadn't caught on, but I loved her for trying.

Now her brow wrinkled, like she was about to ask a question. Then her face relaxed and the question wrinkles disappeared. Her pale gray-green eyes flashed with excitement.

"Cadence Mariah Jolly! That was *amazing*. Wasn't she amazing, Faith? We've got to all try it together!" she said.

Faith looked positively flabbergasted. *Flabbergasted*

was another one of those words that I absolutely adored. It meant really, really surprised. Faith looked surprised and then some.

She remained quiet at first. She simply bobbed her head and said, "Not bad, Mouse." Then she rushed around, pushing us into "our places" and telling us who would sing what part.

Faith took the first verse, then all three of our voices joined together in the chorus. However, even though Faith instructed Zara to take the second verse, when it came time, Zara pointed to me.

"You do it, Moon Goddess!" she said with a grin.

So I did, and again we all sang the chorus.

This time at the end I let my voice sail, and it took off like a kite to Heaven. And I was the only one who could guide it.

I was so swept up in Zara's enthusiasm as she burst into applause again, hugging me tight, that it took a while to realize that Faith had gone still. And quiet.

"Faith?" I said. "Is everything all right? What did you think?"

It was several seconds before she responded. Finally, she said, "How long?"

Huh?

She repeated it. "How long? I mean, how long have you known you could sing like this?"

She looked—*hurt*?

Instantly I started to chew on my lip.

Zara was so into it, she didn't seem to notice Faith. Or the expression on Faith's face.

Zara half turned. "Who cares how long she's known. She's amazing. Maybe we should even let her sing the lead. Oooh! Think about it, Cadence. No one would be expecting it. You could blow folks away!"

I turned to Faith.

She looked dazed.

Confused.

Heat in her stare buzzed electric.

Her body stiff as a winter tree.

Personification. But instead of inanimate objects becoming like people, she was a person who'd gone as stone-still as an object. I wondered if there was a word for that.

"Faith?" I said, softly.

"I think...think that's enough for one day," Faith

said, onomatopoeia-style hurrying toward her coat: *Zoom! Snap! Zing!*

I heard a light knock at my bedroom door, then Aunt Fannie pushed her way in before I could answer.

"Were you girls playing the stereo? I thought I heard Mariah?"

Zara turned to me, and with one desperate look, I silenced her. I said, "We're just trying to figure out what to sing for Mr. Bassie by Wednesday."

Aunt Fannie glanced from one face to the next, her gaze resting on Faith.

"What's the matter?" she asked.

Faith tossed one more look in my direction, then she rushed toward the door. "Nothing. I'm late getting home. See y'all later." Then she was gone.

Aunt Fannie gave us one last long look. "All right, long as you all are playing nice. I don't know who was singing what, but downstairs you all sounded like angels." Then she was gone, too.

I turned to Zara. "Do you think Faith is mad?"

Zara shrugged. "About what? The fact that you're amazing? Girl, she's probably just got a new idea for her own path to fame and fortune," she joked.

Watching Faith rush out of the room without so much as a look back, I had a feeling that Zara was wrong this time. Faith looked angry. At me.

Now I couldn't help wondering:

Would keeping my promise mean losing a friend?

7

I Don't Wanna Cry

I lived through three very awkward school days. Faith was definitely not happy—at least not with me. She was a no-show for practice after school. When I tried to ask what was wrong, she kept saying nothing and I didn't need to worry about her because I needed to be worried about trying NOT to embarrass myself when we finally did have singing practice again. *Humph!*

Just thinking about it made me play my invisible keyboard. Low, eerie notes. Sharp notes with lots of drama.

In Mrs. Reddit's class on Wednesday, she gave us a list

of onomatopoeic words. Soon as she said she wanted us in pairs, everyone partnered up quickly.

"Cadence? You want to choose a partner?" asked Mrs. Reddit, seeing that I was one of the few people left. But before I could answer, Sophie Cohen raised her hand and asked if she could be my partner.

I saw Mei-Mei look over at her. I couldn't tell if she was hurt or not. I did a little shrug, not liking that everyone was looking at us. Mrs. Reddit asked Lavender Winter to partner with Mei-Mei.

It was weird at first, trying to work with someone I didn't know anything about. However, it didn't take long to figure out Sophie was a lot different than Mei-Mei. Talking to her was fun, and she made faces for each onomatopoeia we chose for our poem.

While we worked, I thought about trying to be more of a Moon Goddess and less of a Mouse. I'd already chewed my poor lip until it was practically bruised purple inside. I couldn't even deal with my shyness sometimes. Honestly!

We had cut up tiny pieces of paper and wrote words on each. She pushed some of the pieces around on the table in front of her.

There was an eraser beneath the table where we sat. I pressed the toe of my shoe against it and moved it around. "Sophie, why did you want to partner with me? Instead of Mei-Mei, I mean."

Sophie was new at our school, having arrived shortly after the school year began. She was Chinese, like Mei-Mei. Except when she talked, she wasn't nearly as soft-spoken.

Sophie rolled her eyes and whispered, "My parents adopted me from China when I was still a baby. When we lived in San Francisco, there were plenty of Asians around."

"Like, other Chinese people?" The rubber eraser had rolled away. I stretched out my leg, pointing my toe to try to reach it.

Sophie gave me a look. "China isn't the only country in Asia. There's Japan and Korea, too, even Cambodia."

Her dark eyes looked at me hard. At first, I thought she was about to call me stupid or something wretched like that, but instead, she grinned. "Just messing with you. Yes, other Chinese people, like me. And that is where I was born. But I was raised here in America. Ever since we moved from San Francisco, my mother wants to make sure I have Chinese friends and Chinese study."

She shrugged. "My mother doesn't understand. I was born in China. I don't have to *try* to be Chinese. I just am. She's always putting me with Mei-Mei and even talked to the school, telling them to pair us when possible because we are the same age. And both Chinese. But otherwise, we have nothing in common!"

I stared at her, feeling like *we* definitely had something in common. We both understood what it was like to have people we loved want to fix us. I mean, *honestly*, how do you try to take a Chinese person and make them more Chinese?

Anyway, by the end of the class, we were more comfortable with each other. Especially after she asked, "So you're the one they're giving the birthday party for at the diner, right?" And when I looked like I wanted to throw up from pure embarrassment, she added, "I bet your dad never even asked you if that's what you wanted. Parents can be real jerks sometimes!"

That made us laugh again. Then we were both surprised when Mei-Mei raised her hand and asked to read the poem she and Lavender wrote together.

Lavender cleared her throat and placed one hand behind her back in the way you stand when you're in a spelling bee or getting up the nerve to ask your parents for a favor.

She said, "'A Dragon's Kiss,' by me and Mei-Mei." Then she nudged Mei-Mei, whose head was down and face was covered by a curtain of jet-black hair.

Mei-Mei read, and Lavender began acting out the words:

Clickety-clack! Chomp, chomp, growl.
With scaly hooves, she's on the prowl.

Lavender pounced toward the class. We all drew back, then giggles went round the room. Even Mei-Mei bit her lip as though in fear of unlawful giggling. She continued reading:

She has flaming hot breath and fiery red
eyes
Then spews glowing flames into smudgy
skies.

Surprise.

With that, Lavender jumped toward us, making her eyes bug out. More giggles. Now Mei-Mei's voice was growing stronger, and we were all getting into the rhythm and feel of the poem.

The smoke clears—Poof!

Her skittering tail slithers upon the roof.

Up on the chimney another does grace.
A rattle, then rumble; a fiery embrace.

What you see brings terror.
Monsters lost in their own smoky mist.
Dragons with talons that clatter,
With lips that kiss.

Beware.

When they were finished, we all stood and applauded. Mei-Mei's cheeks reddened, but Lavender, with her blond pigtails and blue plastic glasses, stood tall and proud.

Next was Jones, and he had the funniest poem. He called it "Lunch!"

> *Slurp, slurp, slurp.*
> *Burp.*
> *"Jones! Stop making rude noises," the lunch lady yelled.*
> *Chew, chew. Chomp! Chomp! Chomp!*
> *Chicken nugget day in the cafeteria swamp.*
>
> *"See you later, Alligator." I smacked my lips.*
> *The alligator lunch lady put her hands*
> *on her alligator hips.*
>
> *"Be good, you hear!" she did say. I yelled,*
> *"See you next time on chicken nugget day!"*

Mrs. Reddit threatened that the next time he acted up in class, she would share the poem with Mrs. Koogle, our lunch lady. Who, by the way, did sort of remind you of an alligator.

Of course, I'd written a poem with Sophie. But when she looked at me, I quickly shook my head to keep her from raising her hand.

I don't know exactly how the story of my life would be in a book or a poem, but if it were a song, it would be in the key of *whyyyyyyyyyyyy*. As in, *why* does everything have to be so hard?

♫ ♫ ♫

On Wednesday evening, Zara and I rode to choir practice together.

Practice was at the church in the basement. The congregation had raised money to build a new church, and now we had cool practice spaces throughout the lower level. Zara and I took off for the stairs.

At the bottom step, she reached back and took my hand. "You'll see," she said. "Faith is just... She just needs to get used to the fact that you're a terrific singer. I can't wait till you show Mr. Bassie and Miss Stravinski."

I grabbed her sleeve. "No! Zara, you can't tell anybody. Not yet. I'm not ready. And Faith... I don't know. Please don't say anything. Please?"

Zara bunched up her features. Then she slowly nodded, her long, thick hair moving like a curly curtain. "Okay, Cadence. I promise. I won't say a word."

Since my accidental singing demonstration, Faith had barely made eye contact with me. And she'd had almost nothing to say.

I was nervous about seeing her at church choir rehearsal, but hopeful, too. *Maybe we'll work it out.*

Mr. Bassie led both the Youth and Children's Choirs into the larger practice room. Miss Stravinski was already inside, standing on the stage. To my utter horror, they started sending us onstage in groups.

I looked around, surprised. Still no Faith. Zara turned around, realized what I was thinking, then shrugged. I chewed the inside of my lip. This was definitely history making. Faith didn't miss choir practice.

Mr. Bassie interrupted my worrying thoughts. He said, "Don't panic, young people. This isn't an audition or anything. It's simply a get-to-know-you session. We're putting you in groups, and Miss Stravinski is going to lead you through a couple songs and get a feel for the talent and glory of your voices."

Joya was among the singers in the first group. Her voice, unlike so many others up there, came from deep inside her diaphragm. Her belly. It sounded rich, and the words were as hopeful as church bells. So many other kids were singing from their throats. Mrs. Reddit hated that. "Dig deep," she'd say. "Dig that tone all the way out of your souls."

Miss Stravinski's directing was like nothing we'd ever before seen. She was a small woman, but when the music began to play, she transformed. Facing the singers, her arms flew wide, then snapped shut to the rhythm of the piece.

Swoop!

Swap!

Zip!

She grabbed notes out of the air, tossing signals to the singers, leading their voices up, down. Side to side.

Swoop!

Swap!

Zip!

Her hands flew. Fists pumped. Some kids giggled; other kids hushed them. No one wanted the moment to end—not Joya's singing, not the energetic way Miss Stravinski seemed to tug on the notes and toss them around. You could see Joya's eyes and the eyes of the four other singers onstage with her following the director's assistant, their tones shifting with the sway of Miss Stravinski's body.

When it was time for our group, Zara and I exchanged looks. I did not want to go up on that stage, but I had no reason why I couldn't. I took one last glance behind me, hoping Faith had slipped inside. She hadn't.

Miss Stravinski, only a little taller than Zara and me, wore huge round glasses and had rounded bangs that hung over her face. Still, I could feel her peeking at me. She moved us around, making room, she said, for our voices.

However, soon as we got started, she realized she was one voice short.

Halfway through the song, she stopped Mr. Bassie, who was on piano.

Smiling, she walked toward the risers. Toward me. She said, "Baby, what's your name?"

I thought I said "Cadence," but an explosion of laughter from a group of kids who hadn't been called yet told me I'd said it in my head.

"She don't talk, Miss Lady," said one of the Newton

brothers. The one who liked yanking at the back of my coat and making sounds like his lips were glued shut. I would've liked to glue them shut for real.

When Miss Stravinski looked back at me, my face had turned red. I could feel it. I tried to swallow, but my mouth felt like it was the one that had been glued. Now everyone was staring. A tingle, then the burn of a gazillion hot, pointy needles made me want to crawl out of the room. I tried clearing my throat. Tried taking a breath. I must've looked like I was having a heart attack. The Newton brothers, both of them this time, laughed loud, and several other kids looked down at their shoes like they were embarrassed for me.

And that included little bitty kids in the Children's Choir. It's a sad day when you've embarrassed a bunch of kindergarteners.

If Faith were here, she'd ask everybody what was so funny. She wasn't afraid, not ever. Nothing scared Faith. But I didn't have Faith. Not this time.

Miss Stravinski took a step back. "I didn't mean to alarm you, baby girl. It's fine. You jump in when you're ready," she said.

After that, no matter how hard I tried, I couldn't shake the feeling that everyone was looking at me. Laughing at me. It hurt. Like being stung by wasps. Or stepping on a nail. Or maybe even losing a friend.

♫ ♫ ♫

By the time Friday rolled around, I was happy to have the weekend to look forward to. I could spend as much time alone in my calm blue room as I wanted. I was going to nap and play with Lyra and listen to music. Mrs. Reddit had let me borrow a book by Jack Prelutsky called *My Dog May Be a Genius*. Reading the poems in it had been the only time I'd smiled since being humiliated at choir practice. Faith had made excuses about why she skipped the session. Then she skipped practicing with Zara and me on Thursday, too.

"Maybe we'll have to do it without her," Zara had said, all matter-of-fact.

For some weird reason, the idea of Faith leaving me was like thinking about my mother leaving me. It hurt in a way I couldn't explain. Even if she had been bossy, she looked out for me.

Who was going to stand up for me without Faith?

♫ ♫ ♫

When the time came for kickoff at Junior's football game Friday night, I was beginning to feel better.

It was, after all, the Harmony High School Tigers against the visiting Saints of Bunker West.

The stands were packed. The Bunker West High School band was in the stands across the field. "When the Saints Go Marching In" blared from horns and trumpets. Several of our fans booed cheerfully. Then our band began playing "Eye of the Tiger" and that other song from *Rocky*. I stood at the entrance gate to the field and inhaled the scene.

One of my favorite things to write about was football. I loved almost everything about it. The smell of hot dogs on the grill wafted in the air—air that was chilly and tasted slightly of snow, even though no snow had fallen. Then there were the lights. High above the field. And the way the grass smelled and how the leaves, dry and rough, sounded when a gust of wind sent them jumping along the fence's edge.

"You're going down on the field with your dad?" a voice asked from my side. I spun around, surprised out of my mind to see Faith. I was so happy that she was actually talking to me, my heart almost burst.

"Yes!" I said. "Wanna come?"

Faith shook her head. "Nah, the bands are going to be jumping tonight. I want to be in the stands with our side," she said. Then we both stared at each other, silent as the moon.

She said, "I can't practice this weekend. Really. Mom and Granny June want me to go with them to a craft show in New Castle. We're staying the night. I probably won't be back in time for church. Maybe I'll see you Monday. Okay?"

"You'll still be practicing with me and Zara, though?" I said, even though I'd been afraid to ask.

When she nodded and smiled, I felt a flood of relief. "Faith," I said, voice dropping. I wanted to apologize. I wanted to ask why she'd gotten so angry. Before I could, however, she spun around, waving over her shoulder.

"See you when we get back," she said, running toward the bleachers.

So I said good-bye.

The announcer's voice cut into the stadium noise. I stood just inside the gate to the field, my hands shoved deep inside my pockets, my cheeks and nose cold. He said, "Ladies and gentlemen, as a special treat, we have a very honored guest. This evening, singing the national anthem, is newly signed gospel recording sensation Grace Pendergast!"

Cheers rang throughout the stadium. Shouts of "we love you, Grace!" rose into the night sky.

I spun around and looked for Faith. Sure enough, she was sitting next to Zara with her hands pressed to both sides of her face. Her gaze found mine, and I felt this shiver run through her and right into me. I was so happy that we'd made up. I didn't know exactly what she'd been so upset about, but I promised myself I'd find out.

I didn't feel so separated now. That was the kind of connection good friends shared.

On the field, standing on a wooden box, was an African American girl with curly hair pulled into a bun. She wore large hoop earrings, the thin kind, and a Penn State varsity jacket with jeans and high-top boots.

She waited until the noise died down. I'd edged my way in between several Harmony players and coaches for a better view. I wanted to see.

All the teammates from both sides stood with their hands over their hearts. So did I. Junior looked down, spotted me, then hoisted me onto his shoulders. It was like sitting on the tip of a star.

The girl, Grace Pendergast, began to sing, closing her eyes, her head tilted toward the night sky.

"*Oh, say, can you see...*" Her voice was honey-soft but strong. As she moved through the song, caressing the notes and adding a touch of gospel flare, I could feel the crowd in the stands, both sides, rumbling with their *amen*s and *yes, Lord*s and *sing it, girl, sing it*s.

When she got to the big notes, everybody started applauding. By the time she finished, the spectators were going crazy, the football players were bouncing up and down on the balls of their feet, and I was sure Faith had passed out in the stands.

The craziest thing of all, however, was after the song's end. When she finished, I could have sworn she looked right at me. And winked. Could she tell I was a singer in secret? She wiggled her fingers at me in a little wave, and I waved back.

She was amazing!

Junior knelt and dropped me to my feet. "Thanks, Junior," I said, already running toward the gate.

It was urgent that I speak with Faith instantly to compare notes and see if she loved her favorite singer even more now. When I reached her, she and Zara were sharing a hug. I stood in the aisle hopping from foot to foot.

"Let her in!" cried Faith. Her including me at that moment felt like the best thing in the world.

"Oh, Faith," I began, "I see why you love her so much. She was amazing. Absolutely amazing!"

Zara bobbed her head, making her curls twist and turn in the autumn breeze.

"Grace Pendergast is the real deal," she said. Then she turned to me and said, "But so are you, Luna. Grace Pendergast has more experience, and she knows how to work her voice, but you have one of the prettiest-sounding voices I've ever heard. Right, Faith?"

We both turned to look at Faith, expecting her approval. For me, it was more wishful thinking and not so much expectation. But I could tell Zara just assumed it. Well, we were both in for a big disappointment.

Instead, Faith looked like she'd just fallen off a horse. She put her hands on her hips, and her neck got a bad case of the swivels.

"First off," she said, holding up a gloved hand to tick off her points, "no way can you compare my girl Grace Pendergast to somebody like Mouse. I mean, Mouse sounds okay for somebody who just woke up one morning and decided to actually sing instead of whispering all the time, but still. She is not as good as Grace.

"Second of all, well, maybe that is first and second. I mean, you can't compare her to Grace."

Her. Like I wasn't standing there. Like I didn't have a name. It felt like I'd been punched in the heart.

She plowed on. "And third, what is all this 'Luna' business, anyway?"

I felt myself shrinking so much that I didn't even try to answer. When Zara spoke, her voice was very small. "Her mother once told her she'd wanted to call her Luna, like the Moon Goddess, because Cadence was so fascinated by the moon," Zara said, not getting the story exactly right, but close enough.

Faith rolled her eyes. Then she pinned me with a harsh gaze. "Your name is Mouse. MOUSE!" she practically roared. "I'm not calling you Luna."

I had to get out of there. The game had begun, and the Tigers were moving the ball up the field. Everyone was on their feet cheering as the Tigers quickly got in scoring range. I managed to squeeze out of the bleachers and steal a final look at my friends. Zara stared after me, looking from me to Faith in confusion. I gently shook my head at her and tried to melt away into the sea of screaming fans.

8

There's Got to Be a Way

It was hard falling asleep when I got home. After a while, I gave up, grabbed my journal, and headed for the balcony. Lyra followed. She curled up in a blanket and slept beside my chair.

So quiet and peaceful. Hardly any sounds from cars on the mountain roads, although every now and then, I could hear trucks lumbering in the night.

Cold outside. But my insides boiled hot, and my brain was going wild.

Replay...

Grace Pendergast singing. Beautiful.

Replay…

Her voice casting a magical spell over everyone.

Could I do that?

Would I ever have the nerve?

Replay…

Faith, her words bending with cruelty.

Replay…

My insides squeezing; me feeling weak. Afraid.

Now the fear was gone.

Anger took its place. Now I wondered what it would feel like to be *discovered* as a singer, too. To share my special kind of magic with an audience and feel them loving me with each breath I took.

Which reminded me of our poem, the one by me and Sophie that I begged her not to read in class.

Discovery

"Hush!" said the mountain.
"Shush!" said the gloom.
"I am here," said a girl who was up in her room.

Waiting. And waiting. And…
Waiting.
She sighed.

A mumble and grumble did ~~stumble~~ rumble inside.

"Whisper! Whisper!" said the night.
"I am here!" cried the girl who ~~was~~ hid out of sight.
Waiting for a time when she would stand in the light.
Waiting for the fluttering of her fans' delight.

~~She was~~ Waiting for a time when her soul would be free.

"Behold!" murmured the night.
A discovery!

The poem, its cadence, replayed in my mind. So did choir rehearsal. Especially the part where Miss Stravinski had explained once again about us making our own videos.

"Mr. Bassie and I want each and every one of you to record yourselves and share your recordings with this account," she'd said, pushing her glasses back in place. She said the webpage was private, and only she and Mr. Bassie could access it.

"Also, young people," she went on, walking from one end of the stage to the other, her tiny self trying to look stern, "remember, the winning groups will get to rerecord their videos to show as part of the Gospel Jamboree. And you'll also perform in front of a band, just like the adults. Remember, you are artists, too. Don't let us down."

Remembering made my heartbeat quite fortissimo, which is very loud indeed.

I wished I could be like the main character in *A Crooked Kind of Perfect.* It's about this girl named Zoe

Elias. She wished for a piano, but instead was blessed with a big, clunky organ.

The author was named Linda Urban, and she did a very good job. She helped Zoe find a way to be all right with getting an organ, rather than a sleek piano, with finding her own kind of success, rather than the success of her dreams.

If only someone would come along and do that for me. Zoe had to learn how to find joy in not getting what she wanted. I'll bet she never imagined that getting exactly what you thought you wanted could be trouble, too.

What would Ms. Urban write in a story about me?

I sat on that thought. This stuff was almost too real. Instead, I wanted a little magic in my life.

Lyra stirred beside my chair, then, as usual, climbed into my lap. Rubbing the warm silk of her furry head, I whispered, "I need to figure out a way for Mr. Bassie to 'discover' me. But if I just send him a recording of me singing, wouldn't I seem like kind of a braggy person?" *And what if I'm not that good?*

Frosty night air turned my question into cold mist. Lyra looked up at me with sleepy, warm, brown eyes. She told me the proper word was *braggadocio.* Miss Lyra had a very advanced vocabulary. She also reminded me that I was more afraid of...being afraid! She settled into me, satisfied. I sank back against the chair, wondering what to do.

I grabbed my tablet and switched it on. When it came to life, I swiped quickly to my video account.

A familiar page opened, showing music videos I had saved. The kind of recordings made during church services or at festivals by family members or proud friends and neighbors.

I felt the familiar catch in my throat.

My mother's face came into view.

She was maybe twelve or thirteen. In church—the old one, before the renovation. Standing on the stage, a colorful headband around her short, spunky hair.

The pastor back then is now retired. He introduced her and said, "This young lady is going places, church! A talent like hers comes around once in a blue moon."

*Hallelujah*s chorused.

She began to sing "I Go to the Rock" by Whitney Houston and the Georgia Mass Choir. Voices from the adult choir members enveloped my mother's in harmony like protective wings. Her voice was steady and commanding. She did sound so much like Miss Whitney Houston.

I got the usual lump in my throat as I felt her singing move me.

One after the other, I watched videos of my mother. We used to watch them together. She'd been so proud. Sharing her past. Drawing me into it. Maybe hoping someday I'd have the same gift. Maybe praying that someday, I'd have my own videos.

Then an idea slammed home.

Sudden. Unexpected. It made me gasp. Lyra sat up, more alert than before. I told her my idea. She gave me her best doggie smile. Wagged her tail and sang in her most perfect high C.

Good girl, Lyra. Good girl!

Daddy let me sleep in past our normal Saturday cleaning routine, and when he tried to wake me for breakfast, I told him no, thank you.

Well, of course, he couldn't just take my word that I was tired. He had to lumber over and feel my forehead.

Was I feeling well? Was I coming down with some rare disease that only quiet, motherless girls get? *Oh, Daddy.*

Naturally, I could not tell him the truth. That I'd been up late watching videos of my mother and planning a little discovery of my own.

He forced me to drink orange juice and take two baby aspirins and some vitamins. Then he brought me a cup of mint tea and some toast.

"I'll bring you something back from the diner a little later," he told me. Then he was off to the workshop he shared with a friend to rehab some broken instruments. Daddy really liked that shop. And the funny thing was, ever since he'd fixed up the Takahashi 3000x for me, business had picked up.

Soon as he was gone, I sprang out of bed. Lyra and I twirled.

"We did it, Lyra! We did it!"

Milky daylight washed through the blue plaid curtains and over the calm blue walls. Lyra cast a dark blue shadow against the cool blue rug. I sank onto the floor, pulled the quilt down around my shoulders, and lifted my teacup from the nightstand.

Last night while I was on the balcony listening to my mother's voice, I'd gotten an idea. The videos reminded me of Grace Pendergast and how she'd been discovered—by posting videos of herself online.

Faith was always talking about how much she wanted to upload her own videos and get discovered, too.

Soooooo...

Maybe it would work for *me*, as well.

Only, instead of just posting a recording of me singing, I had something else in mind.

I could post a video on the private YouTube channel Mr. Bassie and Miss Stravinski gave us.

Last night on the balcony, I'd remembered Junior's silly phone app. The one he and his friends used when they dressed up like girls. I sneaked into Junior's room, stole his phone off the charger, then took it outside on my balcony.

I chose the first song that came to mind—"One Sweet Day" by Mariah and Boyz II Men.

It took several tries before I decided I was ready. That was when I began playing around with the phone and accidentally opened Junior's text messages.

Snooping was never my thing. But I happened to see

something that caught my attention. It was a message from someone called 99Wolverine. It read:

Dude, let me know. I'll help if I can

Junior answered:

JR_Hit_emUp: Yeah, man. Let's make it happen.

99Wolverine: Man this ain't no joke at Michigan they go hard for sure/be glad to have you

JR_Hit_emUp: Dad stuck on P State but U-M for Life is whatsup

99Wolverine: Maize and Blue for Life fo sho, will have QB coach call you

I felt a little shudder. So I wasn't the only one with a secret. Junior was hiding something, too. He wanted to play football for the University of Michigan.

My mind flashed to the huge poster on his wall. Some guy named Desmond Howard holding a football tucked in one arm, his opposite arm outstretched. Every Friday, part of Junior's game-day ritual was to fist-bump that poster on his way out the door.

He told me Desmond Howard once played for the University of Michigan. He'd pointed him out one Saturday while he was scarfing down cornflakes, watching one of those talk shows that come on before football games. Desmond Howard was now an announcer on his and Daddy's favorite channel, ESPN.

Junior leaving Pennsylvania to play football? The thought left me panicky. I didn't want him to go. And what about Daddy? I didn't even want to think about his reaction if he ever found out Junior didn't want to play for Penn State.

But of course, I couldn't say anything. Otherwise he'd know I'd been snooping through his phone.

Better to concentrate on one thing at a time.

So I flipped through his screens until I found the right app. Then I tucked the phone itself into a planter, propping it up so it could record me.

I'd stood there, underneath the stars, praying my voice would sound as silky as honey, and began to sing.

The first time, I'd made it all the way to the end before Lyra decided to add her two cents. I usually loved her high C, but not right then.

It took several more tries before it was perfect.

I spent another hour figuring out how to use the filter on Junior's app so that it would hide my identity.

My plan was simple:

1. I'd share the recording to Mr. Bassie's private YouTube channel.

2. He'd see it and be blown away by the amazingness of it all.

3. He'd have to know the identity of the singer!

4. At rehearsal, when he asked who had posted the video, I'd come forward and tell him it was me, Cadence Mariah Jolly. I would tell him I'd accidentally sent it to him. A little white lie.

After watching Internet sensation Grace Pendergast move the crowd the way she did on Friday, then feeling humiliated when Faith sneered at me, I was on a mission.

I didn't want to feel like a downright loser anymore. I wanted to be strong, like Heidi in *So B. It.* A girl who takes action.

I wasn't ordinarily a sneaky person. Part of me, a little, itty-bitty speck of me, thought it would be great if I could just go up to Mr. Bassie and Miss Stravinski and say, "Excuse me, I'd like you to hear me sing."

But I couldn't. Really.

So what harm was there in letting them "discover" me?

I was sure if I revealed that I made the recording, I'd somehow, right in that moment, get the nerve to sing for Mr. Bassie. And he'd help me build up my confidence before singing for everyone. I was really, really sure it would work that way.

Time to walk the dog. I got dressed, leashed Lyra, and headed out into the overcast morning. And I sang. Not just soft, sweet falsetto, either. But big, round, curling notes that sailed off into the sky.

And I didn't care who heard.

Okay, maybe the not caring part was in my mind.

But I did sing.

And it did feel good!

One Sweet Day

Sunday. "You sure seem to be in a good mood," Zara commented as we arrived at church. Instead of the Lodge, we were having our usual Sunday service. Aunt Fannie was doing her fast-walk-in-heels dash. *Click-clack. Click-clack. Click-clack* went the pointy high-heeled boots across the icy-cold pavement. I was beginning to hear onomatopoeias everywhere.

"You girls don't dally," she said. Her voice was a girlish singsong. Her tone dolce soprano, sweet and high. "Get inside. The calendar might say October, but these here mountains are saying winter!"

Beyond the pitched wooden beams of the roof, mountains rose in staggered heights. They wore halos of mist, giving the entire building and the background a storybook feeling.

It looked so peaceful. I sighed. At least knowing that Faith was out of town with her family was a relief. I was still upset at how she'd behaved at the football game.

I imagined how shocked she would be one day to find out I could sing in public, without being afraid.

Inside, we hung our coats and raced to the rehearsal room to go over our song for this week. Jones was singing lead instead of Princess Precious.

His face was scrubbed shiny. His suit coat, complete with pocket square, made him look like a little businessman. And of course, his bow tie.

"I see you ladies are here to sing backup for me," he said. *Honk-honk-honk-honk!* See, just when you start to think he's going to be decent, he goes and Joneses up the place.

Zara and I rolled our eyes and walked away.

Children's Choir members wore white shirts or blouses over black pants or skirts. A few girls wore dresses. My skirt was black with pleats, and my white shirt had a rounded collar. I wore black tights and a pair of new black Mary Janes that Auntie had bought for me. And of course I wore my genuine imitation pearls from Sam's.

As pleased as I was with my Sunday choir attire, I had to admit to a bit of envy. We all did. The Youth Choir had shiny purple church robes with white collars.

All of us longed to one day wear the bright purple robes as a sign of our maturity and utter sophistication. Not to mention, Youth Choir got to travel, compete, and sing at several functions. The Children's Choir sang at church and the Lodge.

My heart was beating fast, but not the frenzied snare drum pace. More like a steady conga beat—a slow, rhythmic tempo. I was so excited about what I'd done.

It was killing me to keep quiet. But then, the whole reason for doing what I'd done had been to not draw attention to myself until the right moment. I'd even erased the video off Junior's phone so he wouldn't know.

In my head I had it all worked out like a great book:

The main character (me) would be heard singing in the video. The music teachers (Mr. Bassie and Miss Stravinski) would hear her voice and wonder who it could be. They would love her voice and decide that some girl in the choir, too shy to come forward, had sent in this video and they simply must find out who she was.

It would be like *Cinderella*. Only instead of a glass slipper, it was an impressive range of octaves from C to shining C. (That's music teacher humor, courtesy of Mrs. Reddit!) Quietly, Mr. Bassie and Miss Stravinski would sneak in girl after girl, getting them to attempt to sing the musical scale. Effortlessly. Mrs. Reddit always stressed that if one had to strain for a note, then the note was not natural for their voice.

The idea was so wonderful that I must have been grinning like a madwoman. Zara nudged me as we shuffled into position backstage.

"What are you smiling about?" she asked.

I shrugged, too caught up in my plan to answer.

However, it had never occurred to me what would happen after I—well, my character—admitted to making the recording. That they might just make me sing in front of everyone right away. How had I jumped over that part?

As it turned out, singing for Miss Stravinski and Mr. Bassie alone would have been a lot better than what really happened.

Mr. Bassie wanted to make an announcement.

After that, nothing was ever the same.

Miss Stravinski led us onto the stage. We took our places. The Children's Choir was performing only one song, "I Believe I Can Fly," by R. Kelly.

There was something about the way Miss Stravinski had arranged the music. How the notes grew stronger and stronger, all the while letting Jones shine. I felt proud singing backup for him, all our voices uniting, soaring, rising. I think I might have actually sung a little louder this time. It felt good being part of the whole, even if I did feel terrified the entire time. No one around me seemed to notice, though.

When the song ended, everyone stood. Jones received a standing ovation. Now, ordinarily I would have expected him to puff out his chest and be all *honk-honk-honk-honk* about it. Instead, he appeared humbled.

We started looking around, preparing for Miss Stravinski to lead us off the risers and backstage.

Only, Mr. Bassie walked out.

"Brothers and sisters, can I get one more round of

applause for this young man!" he said. A spotlight shined on Jones, and the audience piled on more applause. Jones took another bow.

"Hallelujah!" said Mr. Bassie, and the audience and other choir members *hallelujah*ed him right back. The church ladies, including the Trinity, sat together, their colorful hats casting shadows yet their faces revealing the glow of shared joy. I was still applauding when Mr. Bassie continued:

"Ladies and gentlemen, I've had the most wonderful experience this weekend. Sometimes you get unexpected blessings. Well, Saturday afternoon, I got such a blessing from the Internet."

My face froze. And I peeked between the kids in front of me, to follow Mr. Bassie with my gaze. The snare drum rhythm, with its scratchy beat, pelted against my rib cage. Pinpricks of fear danced like fire ants along my arms.

He wasn't about to mention what I thought he was about to mention, was he?

Not while he was onstage.

IN FRONT OF REAL PEOPLE!

No. No. No. No.

Right then, I started praying harder than I'd ever prayed before. *Dear Lord, I know I'm not exactly keeping up with all the favors I've been asking for, but please, please, please, please do not let Mr. Bassie mention the recording I sent—*

Too late.

Overhead screens filled. Floating swirls of pink and red replaced the images of us onstage. (As part of the renovation, flat-screen monitors had been placed throughout the church sanctuary. The Trinity had grumbled that Pastor Shepherd and some of his flock wanted a better way to watch football!)

Next came a voice.

Soprano. Moving effortlessly through the C scale.

My voice.

"*. . . and I know you're shining down on me from Heaven . . .*"

Thank you, sweet have mercy, that I wrapped a long scarf around my head before I recorded myself. The fringes made it look like I had long, thin braids. The app added the swirling colors, so no one could recognize my face—only that the singer was small, probably young, and of course, female.

The recording ended. Gasps and whispered words tumbled around the room like a beach ball in the stands at a football game.

Mr. Bassie rolled his eyes back like he'd just eaten the best, tastiest banana pudding in all the land. He said, "Yes, it's a mystery all right!" Light reflecting off his deep blue suit sparkled like the ocean.

He went on. "I came across this online. A friend of mine in Connecticut called and asked if I'd seen it. He's a choir director, too. He told me he'd discovered this video of a truly gifted young girl singing a cappella. He noticed the YouTube user's location and called to ask what I knew about it."

For some reason, the audience saw this as reason enough to applaud. *No*, I wanted to yell. *Do not applaud. Do Not!*

"Mouse!" Zara whispered. "Is that... you?"

"Shhh!" I hissed.

I must have looked sick because she asked, "Mouse? Oh, sorry, Moon Goddess. You sound amazing, but you are lookin' kinda green. Are you all right?"

I was not all right. Oh, goodness! What had I done?

My chest felt tight, and my face felt hot. I pitched forward slightly. For a second, I really thought I would pass out. Zara was beside me, rubbing my hand. Panic started to bubble inside me.

Mr. Bassie went on and on about how he'd been hoping to find a standout soprano among his young singers. And how he knew the person had to be in our group because of the location stamp.

"My guess is that one of you tried to upload your video to my YouTube channel, but instead you set it as public. Can I get a witness? Hallelujah! Now, I have to tell you, whoever you are, my friend in Connecticut has a big mouth!" he said. Everyone laughed. Except me. I was not laughing.

"If he has his way, by the end of the day, the whole world will be talking about this video. So whatever reason you had for wanting to keep it a secret, whether you're in our choir or would like to be, thank you for the beautiful gift. I'll be looking for you after the service!"

Things managed to get worse.

As soon as we were backstage, voices exploded with the possibilities. Who was she? Who could she be? Was she really hiding in the Children's Choir? Was she older than she appeared in the video? Was she in the Youth Choir?

I felt so dizzy, I stumbled backwards. My face was sweaty. My hands itched. Bethany Joy, our pastor's daughter, stood behind me. She and I used to be really good friends. But that was before my mother left. After that, well, I guess I had motherless-girl cooties.

So I was truly surprised when she walked over.

"Who do you think it is?" she whispered.

I chewed on my lip. Hard.

"Hey, Bethany Joy," Zara said.

Bethany Joy said "hey," but continued to stare at me.

Finally, I said I had no idea who it could be. She shrugged. "Her voice sounds familiar, but I can't place it," she said.

I'd been so caught up in the commotion going on around me and the chill running through my bones that I lost sight of Zara wandering off. Soon as I spotted her, though, I knew something was wrong.

"What's the matter?" I asked.

Then Zara was hugging me, and I could feel anxiousness coming from her body. Had she figured it out already? Did she know my life was ruined?

"What?" I asked, feeling alarmed. "What is it?"

For the first time, I realized she was holding her phone. She waggled it at me. Tears welled in her eyes.

"Zara?" I said.

"Mommy just called. Gran had a heart attack! We have to leave for Ohio right away!"

I felt myself go numb. My arms pulled her tighter. I felt scared and shaken—and ashamed. Because, honestly, I wasn't sure if I was feeling worse for Zara or my sorry self!

10

Heartbreaker

At home later in the kitchen with Aunt Fannie, I hoped keeping busy would take my mind off what had happened. However, all anyone wanted to talk about was that ridiculous Gospel Girl video. Gospel Girl? Who told people they could just go and give her—*me!*—a name? I mean, *really*!

"Oh, Mouse! Isn't it divine? Some little diva in our midst has the voice of an angel. Pass me the carrots if you're done, please, dear," she said.

"Yes, ma'am," I said. The bright orange circles of carrots plinked across the cutting board as I pressed down with a not-quite-sharp knife. Auntie was making dinner tonight. Daddy had invited Miss Clayton over, and Aunt Fannie wouldn't miss a chance to snoop on that for anything in the world. The kitchen smelled of roasting beef and savory blends of onions and carrots and celery.

On Sundays, if you weren't in the den getting ready for some football, you were in the kitchen with the good, good smells and homey atmosphere.

Junior entered through the kitchen door carrying a large casserole dish.

I groaned. "The ladies haven't started after Daddy again, have they?" I asked, low enough so only he heard me. Junior grinned.

"Nah, not unless ninety-three-year-old Miss Moses is trying to get her groove back. She stopped me when I was passing her house. Asked me to bring the old man some of her jerk chicken," he said. Then he said his *how do you dos* to Aunt Fannie and rushed up the stairs. A few minutes later, the house phone rang. I answered it.

"Junior!" I yelled. "It's for you. It's a man!"

Aunt Fannie was still cooking away. "I'm grateful for the jerk chicken, because I know my baby brother has a fondness for it. However, our pot roast is going to be delicious," she cooed. "The butcher gave me one of his best cuts of meat yesterday morning."

She probably scared him with one of her flourishes. Then she asked, "Who was on the phone for Junior?"

I shrugged. "He didn't say. The first three numbers are the area code, right? The part of the country the call's coming from?" Aunt Fannie was the one who had taught me that.

She nodded. "Exactly," she said.

The numbers *734* appeared on the caller ID. That was somewhere in Michigan. I didn't tell Aunt Fannie, but I'd memorized most area codes. That way, if my mother called again, I'd know where she was.

"It's time you learn some family cooking secrets, Little Miss Mouse. And you never did say, who do you think the little singer is? From the video?"

I tried not to shudder. Aunt Fannie was sneaky, but no way was she getting me to talk about Gospel Girl. No way!

Over the next hour, I did my best to mumble one- or two-word answers about Gospel Girl until Aunt Fannie gave up and concentrated on her pie.

A little while later, Miss Clayton arrived. She rapped on the kitchen door and everybody hugged and she asked how things were going. Seeing her outside of school still felt weird. But she looked happy. And Daddy looked happy. So a little weird wasn't so bad.

Aunt Fannie brought out the good tablecloth, white linen and lace, the one we used for Thanksgiving. We set the table and carried in serving dishes filled with steaming pot roast and homemade biscuits, potatoes that I'd personally mashed with real cream and butter, and a huge, steaming dish of macaroni and cheese, Junior's favorite.

"Fannie, everything looks delicious," said Miss Clayton.

"Oh, it looks okay," said Daddy. His BIG friendly voice was less boomy than usual. Maybe he was on his best behavior. Perhaps the meal would not end with him and Junior wrestling each other for the last piece of cake. We did have company, after all.

Daddy slid a glance at Aunt Fannie, making his eyebrows jump up and down, being silly again. So much for good behavior. The more nervous Daddy got, the sillier he became. When he threatened to bring out Sea Bear, I shook my head. He was trying to be playful, I could see it. The way his eyes sort of twitched a little around the corners. The way he tried to control his volume, but little by little, his voice grew louder. Definitely a bit nervous about our guest.

We got down to the meal, and talk between the grown-ups flowed like buttermilk, smooth and easy. I watched how Daddy was with Miss Clayton. She looked nervous, too. Smiling too much, trying to hide her hands in her lap. Sitting next to her, I felt her nervousness jump off her body and onto me. There was something sweet about their awkwardness. They were adorable.

I glanced toward the hallway, down where Daddy's room was. Thinking about his dresser. The photos on it. Pictures of him with Junior; photos of the two of us; and photos of the four of us—Daddy, Junior, me, and my mother.

As they talked and laughed, I glanced around, taking in other reminders of my mother. The rummage-sale painting of a black man playing trumpet, a few rugs in the hallway that she always loved, and of course the coffeepot. Having Miss Clayton in the house made me really see all those little touches. And cringe. It was like we were all part of a story my mother had made up, then left incomplete.

Made me wish they were all gone. I gave a little shudder, not expecting the sudden rush of feelings. Was it aimed at my mother? Daddy? Miss Clayton? Myself? I shook it off.

Anyway, at least no one was talking about Gospel Girl.

"So, Junior, are you thinking about colleges for next year yet?" asked Miss Clayton. She grasped the long-handled spoon and dipped collard greens from the dish. "Pass the cornbread, please."

I passed the cornbread. Junior took a big scoop of candied sweet potatoes. Dribbled juice on the fancy tablecloth. Mumbled "sorry" to Auntie and jumped up to get a wet sponge. Looking over his shoulder at Miss Clayton, he said, "Yes, ma'am. I have a few schools in mind."

Daddy jumped in. "Junior's got one school on his mind: Penn State! That's my boy!" *Boom-boom-boom.* Forte went his baritone—deep and LOUD. Junior seemed to wince. He came back to the table, wiping up the dribbled juice and sliding back into his seat.

Junior made his mouth laugh, but he didn't tell his eyes. He reached for the dish with the macaroni and said, "Yeah, Pop's got it all figured out. No need for me to do anything but show up, I guess."

Boom-boom-boom! Daddy went right on as if he didn't notice Junior wasn't laughing. Daddy boomed, "That's right, boy. I got it all figured out. All you need to do is your job—play good football and keep your grades up. Let me worry about the rest."

Junior scooped his mac 'n' cheese. His baritone matched Daddy's, and his new laugh sounded almost scary. "Yeah, old man, I'll just sit back and let you figure it all out."

I gulped my sweet tea and glanced at Miss Clayton, who was looking at me with question marks in her eyes. I wasn't imagining it. Something was going on between Daddy and Junior. But when I looked from one to the other, I didn't see anger. More like the faces they made when the team was staring down a huge opponent in a Friday football game.

Daddy even called it their "game face." He said you have to put your game face on to concentrate. Block out everything else.

Hmm...so why were they wearing their game faces at the dinner table?

I looked away again, and this time when I looked back, they were both making goofy faces at each other across the table. Being silly, like usual. Maybe I was imagining things. I sighed. My imagination was my best friend, but it had already led me wrong once.

No need to imagine something between Daddy and Junior, too.

We all took our desserts into the den. Banana cake with walnuts and banana cream frosting. My favorite. I got to make the frosting this time; Aunt Fannie had taught me how. But I hadn't grabbed a slice of cake. My stomach felt as unsettled as Junior's harsh laugh.

We settled in for football and yelled at the TV for the Pittsburgh Steelers, cheering when they scored. At halftime, I felt grateful. Everybody was enjoying the game so much, no one mentioned the video or Gospel Girl.

"Daddy, I'm going to walk Lyra, if that's okay," I said.

"Don't go far!" he said, his overprotective radar kicking in.

Miss Clayton said, "Enjoy your walk, sweetie."

Sweetie? It felt really weird to be called "sweetie" by your teacher in your own house.

I asked Junior if he wanted to run alongside me, but he said he had stuff to do. It took only a few minutes to walk Lyra. She wasn't enjoying the cold or the sleet that had started to fall. The storybook mist that had surrounded the mountains earlier had turned to storybook gloom. Frozen pellets of ice pricked my cheeks. Lyra and I both decided we'd rather be warm.

Upstairs in my room, I changed my socks because the pair I'd been wearing had gotten wet from the icy rain.

With that out of the way, I found myself feeling uncertain in my soothing blue room. It wasn't even five in the evening, but already light was draining from the sky. My room was a collection of shadowy shapes in an assortment of blues.

One shape stretched along the back wall like a hulking caterpillar—my books. Collected over time from Sofine and many others in town. I sighed, walking over to the uneven stacks. Then I found my backpack and dropped *So B. It* onto the pile. I picked up the last book I'd gotten from Sofine—*The School Story*, by Andrew Clements. But I wasn't in the mood to read just yet.

The tall, skinny lamp that stood beside my keyboard lit up the room once I twisted its knob. Then I made sure the keyboard was plugged in. The microphone, too. And I began to play. At first, nothing in particular. I pretended I was having a concert, playing a bunch of songs I knew by heart. In a show they'd call that a medley.

"Coming to you, live from the stage, it's the one, the only, Cadence Mariah JOLLY!" I said into the microphone, my voice rising an octave with each part of my name.

Then I focused on the music. I played "Rudolph, the Red-Nosed Reindeer," "Twinkle, Twinkle, Little Star," "Jingle Bells," and "Snakes Go for a Walk," all songs I'd learned before kindergarten. Playing the music made me laugh out loud.

Then I moved to the middle-C songs I'd been playing for a long time, too. I thought of the first song I'd really had to practice. Couldn't do it from memory. So I had to go to my library.

A row of three floor-to-ceiling bookshelves stood against the wall opposite the window. I turned and found the stepping stool. I kept old music on a higher shelf because I didn't use it as often. I balanced on my tiptoes until I found what I was looking for.

When I blew the dust off, it made me cough. Lyra raised her head from my pillow, yawned, and went back to licking her paw. *Gotta remember to change that pillowcase tonight!*

I got the music I was looking for. Canon in D by Pachelbel, though I had learned it in C. In case you were wondering, Canon in D is a song they play at weddings. Not the "Here Comes the Bride" song, but another one that is more beautiful. At least, to me. Canon in D was a beautiful piece of music that made me feel so grown-up.

As I began to play, memories came flooding back. I'd been six when I learned this piece. For a music competition for kids over at Penn State.

Even then, I remembered Daddy talking to Junior about growing up to go to college there someday. Daddy had been singing that tune for a long time.

My fingers found the familiar notes, and the keyboard sang in a perfect harmony. I looked at the sheet of music, staring hard—so hard it was as if I were looking through it. And on the other side of the musical notes, the beautiful melody, the pride I'd felt learning this piece of music at the age of six, was my mother.

Not the mother in my imagination—the real one.

I remember her standing in the wings backstage at the competition. She was supposed to be in the audience, but she'd told them I was so shy I might not play at all if I couldn't see her. I don't know if that was true; I just remember feeling scared and happy and terrified and proud all at the same time.

Everyone had made such a big deal out of it.

There were nine of us little kids. We'd participated in some program or other. Gotten selected for a piano competition. Daddy told me not to think of it as a competition. He told me to just concentrate on playing the best I could.

My mother whispered, "You can do this, Cadence Mariah. You can beat these kids. Just believe in yourself!"

As I continued to play the piece on my keyboard, I shut my eyes, no longer staring through the sheet music, but instead going back inside myself. To the place where I'd had my mother and she'd had me.

And I played Canon in D in the key of middle C.

And I played.

And wetness bubbled in the corners of my eyes.

And I played...and played...and played.

Tears, fat drips of them, fell onto my soft, warm sweatshirt.

I could see her so clearly. She was right there. To the side of the stage. Smiling her proud-mommy smile. And there I was, her quiet little Mouse, playing my heart out. A heart that was pounding in middle C.

Brushing tears off my cheeks with one hand as I continued playing with the other, I lifted my gaze and spotted the trophy. The one I'd been awarded at that competition.

Second Place.

I didn't win.

I didn't win.

Her face had fallen. She'd looked like she was the one who'd lost. Maybe she was. They were all there—Mom, Daddy, Junior. We went out for ice cream afterward. I couldn't eat mine. It had made me sick.

Abruptly, I stopped playing.

A thought settled over me, darker than the charcoal

clouds scudding across the sky. My mother left us because she didn't want to be second best. Why be a mother wishing to become a singer when you can just go out and BE a singer? Especially if you're raising a daughter who doesn't talk and can't even win a kids' piano contest?

I stared out the window. My face felt hot.

I began to play again. Another song I knew by heart.

"O Holy Night." This time, I leaned forward, toward the microphone, and sang, "*O Holy Night, the stars are brightly shi—ning. It is the night of our dear Savior's birth....*"

Don't know why I chose to sing that song. But the words came out, and soon I was singing with all my heart. Pushing away thoughts of second-place trophies and mothers who leave. Pushing away thoughts of Gospel Girl and the trouble she was going to cause me.

"*Fall on your knees...*" I continued the verse, progressing across the do-re-mi-fa-so-la-ti-do scale, feeling the lyrics climb over my heart and pour out through my soul.

Not thinking about mothers or music competitions or children left behind.

Do you want to know how to be stronger? asked the voice in my head.

Do you want people to stop calling you Mouse?

I was almost finished when I noticed something.

On the dresser, right beside my door, sat a slice of cake on a small plate. And a glass of sweet tea.

Had Aunt Fannie come in while I was so caught up in my song that I hadn't even heard her?

". . . O night, O night divine."

11

Fantasy

Zara was gone.

It was Monday morning and Miss Clayton had quietly commented to me about the good time she'd had at our house. Then she told Faith and me that Zara's mom was taking her to Ohio while Zara's grandmother recuperated. "Zara will be doing her studies long-distance for a short while," Miss Clayton said. Zara had already told me. She texted. I'd looked up Ohio on the map app on my phone. She was 158 miles away. Might as well have been a thousand.

If only that had been the worst thing, missing Zara and hoping her grandmother was okay. But no, there was more. Much more.

It started after school. At first, I was so happy. The first thing Faith said to me when we were alone was "Sorry. I can be a real jerk-face sometimes." Then she hugged me and said she was sorry she'd been so mean to me at the football game. And she said if I wanted her to call me Luna, then she would. I hadn't really asked anyone to call me that. It was Zara who'd decided to start that because of what I'd told her.

I cleared my throat, looked straight at my friend, and even though I could feel butterflies tap-dancing in combat boots in my stomach, I said, "Yes, please. I would love for you not to call me Mouse anymore. Luna would be good. Or Cadence."

We hugged and decided to go to the salon after school. "Mama says she needs me to help sweep up the shop. She said you could come, too. I figure if you help, we can go into the basement and sing when we're done."

So it was a plan. I called my Dad at work. He said he'd meet me there later and we'd go get some dinner.

Of course, when we climbed into the car, Mrs. Bettancourt twisted around in the seat to look at me. "Hey, baby, haven't seen you in over a week," she said.

I said, "Yes, ma'am." I smiled. She smiled back. I looked out the window.

Still, I could feel her looking at me. Normally, I'm pretty comfortable with Faith's family. Now, however, Mrs. B. was giving me the willies.

"I'm glad you're coming with us to the shop today," she said. "Wanted to ask you about your birthday present. We want to get something for your party."

I tried not to cringe.

Then she reached into her big purse and pulled out a plastic shopping bag.

"Almost forgot!" she said, thrusting the bag toward me. I looked at Faith. She shrugged.

A book.

The Magician's Elephant, by Kate DiCamillo. I had heard of her. She wrote *Because of Winn-Dixie*. I loved that book.

"Thank you," I whispered, but she had already turned away, looking at the road, wearing a big ol' smile. It was the smile I saw each time someone did a good deed for me—helping the poor little motherless girl. Sometimes that smile by itself was enough to weigh down my spirit.

Once we got to the salon, Faith asked if I'd heard the news. I asked her what news and she got all excited.

"Gospel Girl! You are getting a lot of attention. Mama said she heard them mention it on the morning show. On TV." When Faith said "TV," her eyes started to glow. *Honestly!* Glowing eyes because of a thing like TV.

Reality came back and hit me square between the eyes once Faith's words sank into my brain. I whispered, "You didn't tell her, did you? That it's me, I mean! And, wait, how did you know it was me, anyway?" We were alone in the back of the salon, but she was being so loud. *For Heaven's sake!*

"Of course I didn't tell Mama, Mouse—uh, Luna. Sorry. That's gonna take some practice. Anyway, I've seen the video. Heard the singing. I could tell it was you. And it gave me this great idea. Really great!" she said.

She had the broom. I had the dustpan. *Sweep, sweep, sweep.* Low A, A, A. Low G, G, G.

"What's your idea?" I asked. Background noises

filtered from the front of the shop. Mrs. Bettancourt was talking and laughing with someone. On Mondays the shop was closed. Her grandmother came, along with a few of Faith's aunts and cousins, and helped give the place a good scrubbing. Every week. No matter what.

Faith swept up the last of the trash, grabbed the scooper from me, tossed the trash in the can, and yanked out the garbage bag.

"Mama, me and Cadence are taking out the garbage!" she yelled through the curtain that separated the front of the shop from the back.

"Wear coats!" her mother yelled back.

The dumpster was half a block down, in the alley. The temperature was so cold it felt like the Ice Age, even though it was still October. Of course we were going to wear our coats. Maybe it wasn't just my dad.... Maybe there was some parent thing that made them treat perfectly smart ten- and eleven-year-old girls like tiny babies.

Faith looked around like we were being trailed by trash can spies while we walked to the large green bin, and said, "We should tell everybody that the person singing in the video... is ME!"

I stared at her. *What? Huh? Who? Whaaaaat?*

When the school year first began, Mrs. Reddit would have us do warm-ups for our voices. One was to sing animal sounds. It was soooooo embarrassing at first. Then it got kind of fun.

I stared at Faith. In my mind, I was a confused gorilla, moving up the octave scale:

Whoo, hoo-hoo!

"Faith, that won't work," I said, leaving my gorilla behind.

We had arrived at the big trash bin in the alley. She flung the bag over the top, then she grabbed my hand.

"Look, Mouse..."

I did look at her, then realized she'd already forgotten not to call me Mouse. I wanted so badly to say something to her, but I didn't.

Faith rushed on, "Look. You know I've wanted to be a superstar singer forever, right?"

Many mumbling mice, making mighty music in the moonlight, mighty nice!

That was another warming-up exercise we did. I just knew she was about to cover me in crazy.

Whoo-hoo-hoo.

Many mumbling mice, making mighty music in the moonlight, mighty nice!

She went on:

"So this whole getting-discovered thing means way more to me than it does to you. How would you feel if I turned in some dumb ol' book report in Miss Clayton's class, then she came and told me this book company was going to print it and turn it into a big bestseller?"

I froze. The very idea of Faith as a No. 1 Bestselling Author of Amazing Stories when she didn't even like to read—well—I would die. I would simply die!

She gave me a look that said, *Thank you!*

Then she said, "And in the video, you must've had something on your head, because instead of seeing your short hair, it looks like you have long hair. Long braids. Like me."

It made me ache, knowing my reasons for doing what I did. All of a sudden, I thought of the little story I'd been building in my head earlier, the one about being onstage, as well as the story I'd been building for much longer. The one about singing with my mother.

Would they ever be more than that?

I wiggled my scarf at her. The fringes danced in the wind. "I'm wearing this around my head in the video. The fringes are really long," I said.

Just then, her mother stuck her head out the door, gripping a long sweater tight around her body.

"Whatever girl gossip you need to do, come and do it inside, my darlings!" her mother said, the wind kicking up, throwing dried leaves and twigs like daggers. She looked out past us at the swirling autumn and said, "Snow is coming."

As we passed her in the doorway, she planted a warm kiss on each of our faces. When I saw how she looked at Faith, I could feel the love and pride and honor. Then she looked at me and had a different smile. Not the pity smile, though. Something else.

Lifting one eyebrow, she said, "How about you let me do your hair for your birthday party? Something sassy. Your payment for helping out! My gift to you!"

She always did my hair for free. I sighed. My cheeks flushed pink and warm. I said, "Yes, ma'am. Thank you!"

"We're going in the basement. Um, to fold towels,"

said Faith, yanking me toward the stairwell before I could say another word.

Once we were down there amid baskets of unfolded towels, salon capes, and dust bunnies, Faith swung around and said, "So, anyway, my idea!"

♫ ♫ ♫

For the next hour and a half, we set about trying to figure out how to make her idea work.

Faith figured out I'd used a phone app to create the illusions that hid my identity. She figured we could reshoot the video without a filter, but this time she'd lip sync those parts and make it look like I'd been in the background while she sang.

I tried telling her it was nuts. It wouldn't work. Everyone knew she couldn't move up and down the scale or hold her high notes. Only, Faith insisted that she'd been practicing and had a secret of her own. Then she let loose an earsplitting collection of notes that rose higher and higher until she rested at the low soprano range.

"Faith, I don't know about this," I finally said.

"But Mouse, this is my dream. The kind of attention

you're getting. Or would be getting if you weren't hiding. I've always wanted that."

Luna. Call me Luna. Or Cadence. Or Miss Adventure. Anything other than Mouse.

Whoo-hoo-hoo!

Many mumbling mice, making mighty music in the moonlight, mighty nice!

No way did I want anything to do with her scheme, but she was so sincere. And she'd made a good point about how I would feel if she were the author and not me, I guess. Although, she made it sound like having two dreams would make me greedy.

I looked at the ground, not knowing what to say.

"Please!" she said.

I felt something in my soul start to crack.

Maybe she was right.

Was I a bad friend to have a talent that my friend wanted for herself?

Or was fate trying to tell us something else?

12

Don't Forget About Us

Daddy picked me up at the beauty salon right on time. We were going out to eat before he dropped me at choir rehearsal, where I was meeting Faith. I could tell that Daddy noticed something was going on with me. I caught him giving me the side-eye stare in the car. "Feel like Chinese?" he asked. I shrugged, because he knew I always felt like eating Chinese food. He zoomed past the Big Orange Diner and went down the block to Chin's.

"Are you going to tell me what's wrong?" he finally asked when we were inside the restaurant, seated at a booth with red vinyl seat covers. Tiny candles flickered from each of the tabletops. Shadows danced around the room like ghosts.

I shrugged again, and he said, not in a joking voice but a Daddy voice, "Please stop doing that. Could you answer the question?"

This time he got a sigh instead of a shrug. Finally, I decided if I couldn't tell him what was really on my mind at the moment, I'd settle for the next best thing:

"Daddy, do we have to have a big community birthday party this year?" My face felt hot and tingly just asking. And the minute I saw the hurt expression in his eyes, I wanted to tell him I didn't mean it. It was like the time I'd broken a fancy-looking perfume bottle my mother left behind. While we swept up the glass together, he'd told me he didn't mind, it didn't matter, but one look at his sad face, and you knew he was telling tales.

I rushed on. "Some of the kids have started making fun of me, you know, because the whole town gives me a party. They're calling me Little Orphan Annie." More than once, I'd overheard kids in the hallway or in the cafeteria whispering about me.

Okay, it was only a couple of times. And they were only whispering about how they felt sorry for me or how their parents felt sorry for Daddy. I think, deep down, it might have felt better if they had been really mean and awful to me. At least then I could get angry. When people pity you, how do you fight back from that?

A noise at the edge of the table caught our attention. Mei-Mei was bringing us glasses of water. And Sophie Cohen was right beside her! She was carrying bowls of crunchy wonton strips.

Daddy reached out and grabbed his glass of water, taking a long drink. I looked at Sophie like *what are you doing here??* and she made a face and mouthed, "Save me!" I almost laughed out loud.

Daddy was saying, "...foolishness. They must be jealous." I realized he was talking about my pity party. The laugh died in my throat like a day-old donut. Instead of balloons, maybe I'd bring my keyboard and play the funeral song "Taps."

He went on:

"Sofine and everybody at the diner love doing this. I told you, Mouse, your mama leaving brought out the mama feelings in a lot of folks." I shut my eyes, trying to keep myself from screaming and screaming. Why did he seem to care so much more about what everyone else thought than about how I felt?

"You'll see," he said, grabbing a fistful of wonton strips. "Your party will be a lot of fun. We'll have plenty of people there, and you'll get lots of gifts. A young girl like you needs friends. Needs to be around people. You'll see."

Of course, the whole moment was interrupted. Another loud football talker.

"Jeremiah!" the man boomed.

"Hey, man, how you been?" Daddy boomed in return.

Next thing you knew, Daddy was booming along in one of his football talks. *The Tigers are this. The Tigers are that. Yes, Junior is doing well. Yes, this is Junior's last year. Yes, Junior is on track to go to State.*

Boom. Boom. Boom.

I looked around the room. If I wrote "save me" in the condensation on the window, I wondered, who would come to my rescue? With my luck, it'd probably be Jones. *Honk-honk-honk-honk!*

Instead I focused on the large fish tank right beside

our booth. Some fish were so colorful, shades of bright orange flecked with inky black, while others were a pale, translucent white, their tails rippling in the water. It made me think about Zara. I wondered if her grandmother was doing better. I sent her a quick text.

Mrs. Chin appeared at our table. She spoke to my father and his loud friend and asked how we were. Then she told us the specials, and we ordered. The loud friend had scooted into the booth next to me.

"You by yourself?" Daddy had asked. "Come on, sit with us!" He wore his big, goofy smile, the one that told the world he was happy and not at all sad that his wife had left him with a son and a mousey little girl.

"Your order will be here soon," said Mrs. Chin in her clipped Chinese accent, thin lips smiling.

Soon as she was gone, I saw Sophie in the shadowy hallway that led to the bathroom. She was doing a frantic version of the "come-here" gesture. At me!

"Daddy, can I go talk to her?" I said, trying not to point. "She goes to my school."

He craned his neck around to see, then nodded. "Don't go far," he said.

Can't help himself, I suppose.

His loud football-talking friend grunted as he slid from the booth to let me out. But I couldn't get away before the man called, "Hey, there, Little Miss Mouse, you gotta give me a hint 'bout your birthday. It's coming up soon!"

Grrr!

I so wanted to be the Mouse That Roared. But I just did my usual whimper and rushed away.

"Save me!" Sophie whispered, the loudest whisper a whisper could be, soon as I walked over.

She was looking around from side to side. So I did it, too.

"Save you from what?" I whispered back. Already I felt my mood getting lighter. Sophie was funny, and I liked her. Even though most kids at school thought she was shy, she really wasn't.

She said, "From Mei-Mei and her mom!"

I frowned. "Why are you hiding from Mei-Mei?"

She grabbed my arm and tugged me deeper into the shadows. The bathroom door flew open, and a large woman with a hook nose came rushing out like the toilet was chasing her. She glared at us. Sophie waited till she passed.

"I told you before, my mom is on this trip about me needing to spend more time with Chinese people so I can 'know my culture.' It's so beyond annoying!" When she said "know my culture," she did the thing with her fingers, making quotes around her words, and made her voice sound annoying.

"But Mei-Mei is nice," I said, because I didn't know what else to say. And because I thought it was true.

Sophie rolled her eyes. Now her whisper was gone, and she was talking more regular.

"Mei-Mei is a robot. And her mom is worse. One of those moms who think their children just have to be the best at everything. Some people call them tiger moms. Mei-Mei is a straight-A student, but her mother is pushing her all the time to be better. My mom is Jewish. She believes that even if her kid grows up to be a murderer, you can fix it with hugs and a nice warm meal!"

Her face grew more animated as she talked. The flickering candlelight sparkled in her dark eyes. The dining room was half-full. Conversations mingled together like background music. Every so often, the ting of silverware against china rang out, trilling A notes.

"I guess you're having a hard time telling your mother how you feel," I said. Unlike Sophie, I was keeping my voice down.

She looked at me like I had two heads and webbed feet.

"Are you kidding me? I tell her all the time. She just hugs me, offers me more cake, and says one day I'll thank her! Well, I won't thank her. Mei-Mei is a big bore. I'm tired of coming over here to be her mother's slave for a few hours. Tired of taking violin with her and learning proper Chinese with her. I have no plans to live in China. I'm an American!"

She finished her big speech with one hand over her heart like she was about to recite the Pledge of Allegiance.

Sophie looked so official standing there with her back straight and her hand over her heart that we both burst out laughing, holding our stomachs. Gosh, it felt good to laugh.

Until the bathroom door flew open again.

This time it was Mei-Mei who came out.

Both Mei-Mei and Sophie had dark hair, except Sophie's was long in a ponytail and Mei-Mei's was short. It wasn't their hair that caught my attention, however. At that moment, Mei-Mei's eyes were dark and hard.

And red.

She came over to us, and I wanted to curl up and jump into the fish tank. I should've known better. I had never been friends with her, but I didn't want to make her cry.

Well, she wasn't crying. She was mad.

She shoved her small hands against her tiny hips, looked up at Sophie, and got right in her face.

"You think I want to be friends with you? You think I don't know I have a pushy mom?" she hissed.

Then she said something in Chinese. Fast. Hard to hear and impossible to understand. Mei-Mei took a step back, then glared at us.

"I'm so sorry, Mei-Mei. I didn't mean to hurt your feelings," I said, wishing I could melt away.

She ignored me, still staring at Sophie. "I hear it all the time. Working here while other kids go out and have good time. Me? With my crazy mom, what do I do? I get straight As, that's what I do. I play an instrument, that's what I do. I'm a good Chinese girl because that's what everyone expects. That's what I do. If you don't want to be my friend, then fine with me. I did not ask to spend time with you, you know!"

I had known Mei-Mei since first grade. She had just said more words in a few seconds than I'd heard her say in four years.

Sophie put her hands on her hips. She said, "Well, sorrrrrrr-eeee! No need to get so touchy!"

Mei-Mei flung out another string of Chinese that neither Sophie nor I understood. Then she said, "You are lucky. You only come here for a few hours a week. You help out. You learn our ways. Then you get to go home and be American Sophie. You think I don't want to be American Mei-Mei? I wish I could just be American and watch TV and take dance lessons if I want or no lessons if I don't. But that is not the Chinese way."

"The American way's not always so hot, either," I said in a small voice. Both girls turned to me as if suddenly remembering I was even there. I went on, "I have a big American dad who thinks he has to protect me from everything. Thinks I'm such a mouse that I need the whole town to feel sorry for me. Just because my mother left and is probably never coming back."

I paused, not sure why I was pouring my heart out in the shadowy back hallway at Chin's Chinese Restaurant, but unable to stop myself.

"Everyone in town looks at me and sees a sad girl who is too shy to speak. Probably still traumatized because her mother left. And you know what? I'm not quiet because I'm traumatized. I'm quiet because I just am. I like spending time alone and reading books and listening to music when I want. And when I'm ready for friends, I like hanging out with them, too."

Mei-Mei was nodding her head. "I know you don't like it when people whisper all the time about your mother and where she is. My mom thinks you're so sad. She lights a candle for you at church sometimes."

My mouth dropped open. I hadn't known Mrs. Chin was praying for me. Since they didn't go to our church, I hadn't even thought they belonged to one.

She went on. "I've told her, she's a good girl, Mama. She gets good grades. She's just quiet. She tells me, nonsense. A girl needs her mama. She doesn't even know you!" Mei-Mei made a sound in her throat like she was beyond disgusted.

I knew how she felt.

"Now I have to get ready for a birthday party I don't even want. I call it my pity party. I want to have my birthday dinner here. But do you think my big American dad even cares? No, he's just planning his big pity party, and I'm the guest of honor!"

Whew! I guess that's been building!

Mei-Mei's shy face softened, and she smiled.

"I wondered if you liked those parties," she said.

I shook my head, feeling like a weight had been lifted off my soul. If Daddy wouldn't listen, at least I'd finally found someone else, aside from Zara, who would. Two someones.

Out of nowhere, Mrs. Chin appeared.

"Miss Mouse, your father says come back to the table. Your dinner is ready," she said. Then she slipped her hand inside the pocket of her apron. "Miss Mouse, I want you to have this. Mei-Mei read it; now you can," she said, handing me a book. *The Thing About Luck*, by Cynthia Kadohata.

She turned to Mei-Mei and said, "Table fifteen needs water!"

I thanked her for the book, and when I looked back, saw Mei-Mei and Sophie trying not to laugh. Funny thing—I was trying not to laugh, too. Maybe sometimes life was like that: So weird and messed up, you had to laugh.

13

Shake It Off

Excitement pulsed from the rehearsal rooms and into the stairwell. Something about it made me pause with dread. The air was crackling around me. My heart started pounding. Something was going on.

"Mouse!" Faith came running to the stairs, practically yanking me out of my shoes.

"Uh-oh. What's going on?" I asked. Instantly, all the happy feelings that I'd had in the restaurant began melting away. She was up to something. I could feel it.

She started pulling me toward a quiet corner. Teenagers

and not-quite teens were running around from one rehearsal spot to the other. Miss Stravinski was walking briskly past, then glanced our way and stopped.

"Cadence?" she asked.

The hot ant dance started again. Did she know? What if she knew and was about to tell everyone? I looked at Faith. For the first time I could remember, Faith seemed as scared as I felt.

"Yes, ma'am?" I said, my voice nearly a whisper. At least this time I'd been able to answer. My face still burned hot when I thought about how utterly and completely dumb I must have looked that first night at rehearsal.

She smiled. "Miss Betty told me what an amazing pianist and keyboard player you are. I'd love to have your help today, as we have lots to go over. Oh, by the way, do you think you could play 'One Sweet Day'? I have the music. It's the song by—"

"Mariah Carey and Boyz II Men," I said, automatically. "Yes, I know how to play it." My heart pounded wildly. No more snare drum. Uh-uh. This was a full-on marching-band drum line.

"Yes! Well, Mr. Bassie and I thought it might be nice to have the Youth and Children's Choirs practice it. We're not sure, but we believe the little Gospel Girl whose video is blowing up all over the Internet is either in one of the choirs or in the church. Anyway, you girls hurry up. We're almost ready to get started."

She raced off, almost sprinting.

Faith grabbed my wrists. "See! That's what I wanted to tell you. You know my sister Mercy? The one in high school? She said that video is about to blow up because it's getting so many views." Oh, my! *So many views?* I'd been too afraid to check.

"Mouse," she said, clearly having forgotten all about Luna, "pretty soon everybody's gonna want to know, who is Gospel Girl?"

She leaned in, whispered against my ear, "When people find out, wouldn't you rather they thought it was me instead of you?"

♫ ♫ ♫

All through rehearsal, practicing the very same song I'd recorded, disguised, and uploaded ACCIDEN-

TALLY to the whole Internet, I kept thinking about Faith's question.

Would I rather they thought it was her?

I mean, it would be the easy way out.

But...no. I didn't think I would want anyone thinking it was Faith. Somehow it felt wrong to admit it. I didn't want to hurt her feelings.

I just didn't know what to do.

♫ ♫ ♫

Miss Stravinski started rehearsal with an announcement.

Drumroll, please.

"Mr. Bassie and I wanted to let you know that two of your members have now been promoted. As of next Sunday, Bethany Joy Shepherd and Abraham Jebediah Jones will participate with the Youth Choir."

Applause.

"Miss Betty told me it is a proud moment for you young people when you make the successful transition from Children's to Youth Choir. So, Bethany Joy and Mr. Jones, please come forward and accept your choir robes."

Onomatopoeias popped into my head.

Robes rustling, folded in plastic sheeting.
Shoes scuffing the tiled floor.
Awe in the faces of the rest of the choir.
Shush-shushing sleeves
as robed Youth Choir members applaud.
Congratulations! Congratulations!
Folding around the new members.
They are led by their new choir to
their rehearsal space across the hall.

Right then, more than anything, I knew.

I wanted to be over there, too. I wanted Youth Choir robes for me, Zara, and Faith!

Miss Stravinski broke into my thoughts by asking me to join her onstage. She had me sit at the piano bench, and soon we were under way.

It didn't take long to figure out what she was doing. Sneaky, sneaky, Miss Stravinski. Pretty soon, the rest of the kids figured it out, too. She was trying to put the kids in different groups to tell who might be Gospel Girl.

She asked Faith to sing a verse alone. I almost fell off the piano bench. And you know what Faith did?

"Um, my throat is sort of scratchy tonight," she said.

Then she followed that up with an expression that made her look timid, as though she were afraid of the attention.

Well, honestly!

♫ ♬ ♫

Choir rehearsal ended. Faith's parents came, and Daddy texted to say he was on the way. Miss Stravinski had gone into the Youth Choir rehearsal, and I was alone in the practice room with "One Sweet Day" ringing in my ears.

When I was sure no one was around, I sat in the small space, filling it with music. I drew a deep breath, sat up straight, and relaxed my hands the way Mrs. Reddit had taught me. On a steady exhale, I began to sing. And sing. It felt good, too. Really good. Still…

Something was missing.

I thought about how I'd felt watching Aunt Fannie sing. Then remembered how it felt blending my voice with Zara's and Faith's that first time.

Then I knew.

What I was missing was people. Someone to share the music.

When I listened to my Mariah Carey playlist over

and over and over, her voice took me on little journeys; it comforted me when I felt down; it saved me from the negative voices in my head; and it filled the silence of a phone that almost never rang with calls from my mother.

When I listened to gospel music, it was the same way. Only, I was starting to see that one of the great things about listening to music at church was the fact that I wasn't alone. Maybe the reason I loved going to the Lodge so much for Sunday Brunch wasn't just the kind of music or how good it was.

Maybe it was sharing that music with my friends and family. The good, happy feeling the songs left in my soul all week through.

I'd only ever thought about how the music touched me. Now I was beginning to understand how much more powerful it could be when shared.

Was I really going to help Faith trick the entire church? I continued playing, and singing, letting the conflict and confusion swirling through me come through in the song.

The sound of a door creaking made me stop short.

Mr. Bassie, standing at the rear of the room.

When I stopped playing, he was looking at me. I felt like melting into the floor.

Was this it? Had he heard me singing? Did he know?

"Miss Jolly, your father is upstairs," he said. "Don't forget your things."

He waited for me and ushered me out. He never mentioned hearing me. As outgoing and upfront as Mr. Bassie was, I was sure that meant he hadn't heard me singing, only playing.

As I left the church and climbed into the car, I wasn't sure whether not being found out was a good thing.

Or not.

♫ ♫ ♫

At least I was enjoying poetry class. It was the one place I could go where I didn't have to worry about all the Gospel Girl drama. No Faith. No choir. Mrs. Reddit was all business about our poems.

On Thursday, we were discussing poetry forms. Short poems. Funny poems. Nature poems. Personal ones, too.

She gave us an assignment: to shut our eyes and just

think about how we were feeling. At first there were giggles and squirming. You know how kids are. Then we settled down. I felt the thoughts sitting on me, pressing into me. What was on my mind? What was troubling me? Then I began to write:

The Moon

My mother went away

One day,

Now she lives inside the moon.

I'll take a rocket ship

Someday.

I hope to see her soon.

Then I shocked everyone by volunteering to read it aloud. Well, maybe not volunteering, but when Mrs. Reddit asked me to read it, I only turned sort of red before saying yes.

Jones quickly ran to the piano and began to play. He chose a slow melody that fit the mood of the words.

I felt proud as I stood in front of my classmates, even

though my knees were shaking, and listened while they clapped, then talked about the poem.

"I'm very delighted with you, Cadence," Mrs. Reddit said.

A tap on my shoulder made me turn around.

"Jones!" I said.

Instead of his usual goofy expression, he was staring at me. Really staring.

I felt my cheeks redden.

"What?" I asked, wrinkling my brow.

He took a step back, narrowed his eyes, then a smile started spreading across his face.

"It's you, isn't it?" he said. "It's you. *Ooowee,* Mouse. You're Gospel Girl!"

14

Vanishing

I felt like my life was flashing before my eyes. For sure, destiny had caught up with me.

He followed me into the hallway outside Mrs. Reddit's room. My heart raced. My knees got soft and wobbly.

"No, I'm not!" I'd said.

But he just kept on saying I was. After lunch, when we went back to class, Miss Clayton shooed him away. At recess, Jones came up to me again. Faith saw how shaken I looked and came over. We told her what was going on. Jones said he knew it was me, but I kept denying it.

That was when Faith hissed in an angry whisper, "You don't know anything, Jones. That wasn't Mouse. It was... *me*!"

Unfortunately, Jones being Jones, he looked her up and down, then burst into laughter.

"No, it's not! That Gospel Girl singer is not you, Faith Bettancourt."

A super-huge nuh-uh, uh-huh battle began between them.

Is too.

Nuh-uh.

It is!

No!

Uh-huh!

Nuh-uh!

Then Faith said, "Tell him, Mouse. Tell him how you helped me make the video. Tell him how hard I've been working. Tell him you know it's me!"

So I did. My voice was a shaky whisper. "Um, it is, uh, her, Faith, I mean." I didn't even sound convincing to myself.

Jones's face fell. He shook his head and walked away.

♫ ♫ ♫

Hours later, the lie replayed over and over in my head like a bad music video. Dropping onto the balcony floor, I leaned back against the wall, ignoring the cold seeping through my PJs. I whipped out my iPad and went to my saved videos.

One after another, I replayed videos of my mother at different stages of her life. Singing toward the skylight in the church, aiming her voice at the clouds above a summer festival, dressed in holiday attire and leading a small choir at Christmas. Always her voice, crystal clear and full of emotion.

I wrapped my arms around myself. Cold crept up my legs and through my clothes. Still, I sat, replaying the videos over and over. Wondering what my mother had been thinking of during each performance—those that came before and after I was born.

Then, in one of the last videos she posted while she still lived here, I caught a glimpse of my father. He was standing off in a corner, almost completely out of the shot. I touched the screen and zoomed the image. I saw his face. Whenever I thought about Daddy and my mother together, I'd always remembered them smiling, happy, in love.

However, when I stared at the screen, my father's face came into sharp focus. Tension tugged at his features. He chewed his lip. His gaze searched my mother's face the same way mine searched the night sky—both of us looking for answers we'd probably never find.

♫ ♬ ♫

One week before my birthday, Daddy had a surprise for us. He did something he practically never did—woke up Junior on a Saturday morning.

He told us to get dressed. We were driving over to State College to meet someone. It was a big secret. Junior, normally so easygoing, seemed to really not want to go. Finally Daddy yelled at him and told him to move his butt and get dressed.

What was that all about?

We were heading down the stairs together—I'd been hanging out on the second-floor landing, hoping to catch Junior before he got downstairs with Daddy.

I asked him, "What's going on with you? Have you told him? You know? About not wanting to go to Penn State?"

He didn't look surprised. He knew that I knew. "You tell him you're Gospel Girl? Stay out of my business!" he yelled.

I gasped. He waggled his phone at me.

Now I was getting worried.

In all the time we'd lived together, since I was a baby, Junior had never, ever yelled at me. Not one time.

The crawly ant sensation itched at my skin. I hated to admit it, but I'd been so caught up in the whole choir thing that I hadn't been paying much attention to Junior. It had been over a week since we'd even run together.

The ride to State College took about half an hour. The landscape whipped past like slides on a camera. Some trees had already been stripped bare, thanks to frosty air and high winds. Others sported leaves in deep shades of purple and gold and red. When we arrived at the college campus, Daddy listened to instructions from the GPS.

"In two hundred yards, make a left," the voice directed.

I was sitting up front because Junior had gotten in back. No one had spoken a word the entire ride. Still, when I glanced over my shoulder, Junior was looking at me, frowning. Daddy knew this campus inside and out. He never used the GPS. Why now?

As we were about to park, the radio announcer said, "Hey, everybody, it's your main man, DJ Biscuit. Well, y'all, looks like we've got ourselves a great little mystery brewing in PA. Check this out. How many of you have heard this girl..."

That was when I heard my very own voice playing on the radio.

DJ Biscuit was saying how the local TV morning show *Good Morning, Western Pennsylvania* was trying to identify the young lady singing the cover of "One Sweet Day."

Somehow I managed to slide out of the car and get to my feet without falling on my face. I felt wobbly. I glanced around and caught Junior staring at me. His expression was hard, and for a second, I felt like I saw the same look on his face as I'd seen on Jones's. Disgust and disappointment.

I breathed a sigh of relief when Daddy shut off the car. When I looked back at Junior, he was already striding out of the parking garage, heading toward daylight.

♫ ♫ ♫

We met with three men at brunch. One had icy blue eyes and white hair. His name was Mr. Noble. He said he was the athletic director for the college. The other two men worked with Mr. Noble. It didn't take more than a minute to realize Daddy had cooked up his own secret—a meeting between Junior and the athletic program.

We sat around talking about Junior. How he was doing in school. His social life. His hobbies. Daddy patted Junior on the back and said, "He's a good kid, sir. Well-rounded. Plays the guitar in the church band, and he's got more than twice the volunteer hours he needs to graduate."

Junior smiled a lot, although he looked uncomfortable with Daddy laying on the praise. After the men finished talking with Daddy and Junior, they invited us all to walk around campus. When we got to the creamery, even though it was a chilly day, the line stretched down the street and around the corner. No one complained. Fans had arrived early for a late-afternoon football game. And no one came to State College without making a trip to the Berkey Creamery ice cream shop.

Penn State is one of the few places in the country where you can go to college and major in ice cream. Imagine going to college and majoring in ice cream! The entire time we waited, Daddy and Mr. Noble continued to talk, asking Junior questions and getting him to talk about his life.

From there we got ushered into the stadium's VIP seating, where Daddy and the other men continued to talk with Junior about what it might be like to come to school and play football.

Junior said nothing.

Nothing.

Nothing.

Until I guess he just couldn't say nothing any longer.

"What right did you have going behind my back like that, Dad? Huh? This is supposed to be about me!" Junior was practically barking as Daddy steered the car toward our street.

My face was hot, and my insides were even hotter. Not with anger.

With fear.

Daddy had been going on and on in his jokey way about how great everything had gone, booming about what a good time we'd had. You could tell he meant it, too. It had been a long time since I'd seen Daddy so excited.

Then Junior finally said he was so glad Daddy had had a good time, because he had felt like an idiot.

We pulled into our driveway.

Daddy screeching the car.

Pointing his finger.

My heart pounding.

Junior glaring.

"I've never met anyone so selfish and ungrateful in my life!" Daddy yelled, twisting to point his finger at Junior. "I did this for you!"

Please stop fighting!

Please stop fighting!

Please stop fighting!

I'd never seen either of them so upset. Not even when

my mother left. That had been pain and loss and hurt. We'd held one another together. This was dark and twisted, the kind of thing that rips you apart.

This was hot, red rage. Spewing like lava.

Daddy stalked off toward the house. I sat in my seat, stunned. Junior remained in his seat, too.

Jaws clenched.

Fists tight.

Darkness in his eyes.

Finally, I turned around, and said, "Junior? Maybe you should tell him."

"What?" he snapped.

"About Michigan. About, you know, where you want to go to college."

He reached out and jerked the handle on the door. He looked at me and snarled, "Maybe you should mind your business, Mouse. You've got your own little secret, right?"

Then he stalked off, too.

The heat inside our house clashed with the cold air on our skin. Tiny beads of sweat broke out instantly on Daddy's forehead. I clawed at the scarf around my neck, feeling like I was being squeezed to death by a fuzzy python. Angry sparks flew back and forth between them like shiny knives with pointy, deadly blades.

I tried to make myself small.

"We're not finished with this, Junior. Don't you walk away when I'm talking to you!" Daddy turned to face Junior, who was heading for the stairs.

Junior said, "What else is there to say? You want to choose my school, choose my future, plan my life. When do I get a say?"

"I know what's best for you!" Daddy said.

"Me? You don't even know what's best for you."

"What is that supposed to mean?" Daddy said.

Junior, practically panting.

Me, shrinking.

Desperately, desperately shrinking, smaller and smaller and . . . smaller.

Junior's voice turned from fire to ice.

"What about you and the teacher, Dad?" he said.

Now Daddy's voice had turned icy, too. "What about me and the teacher?"

Junior continued, "I'm not a little kid, man. I got eyes.

Three weeks ago you were driving around, smiling, whistling, wearing new clothes. Now look at you. I know you haven't called her in about a week. I know you've been avoiding her calls."

Now it was my turn to look at Daddy, mouth open.

"Daddy? Is that true? I thought you liked Miss Clayton." How had I missed it?

"Mind your business, boy. That is none of your concern," he said, answering Junior, but completely ignoring me.

Junior's eyes were glassy and shiny, like when you have a fever.

"My BUSINESS? MY BUSINESS?" Now Junior was yelling something awful. Even Daddy, with his face twisting in hurt and anger, took a step back.

"You know what's my business? Cady Cat is my business. My little sister who can't move on from a mama who couldn't be bothered to be a mama. At least my mama stays in touch. She left me with you because y'all agreed I'd be better off with you, right? She calls me three, four times a week, right? What about Chantel? You're all in my business because you don't have any business of your own. Take care of your own business! Stop waiting for someone who is never coming back. Someone you shouldn't take back even if she did!"

It was playing out like a story in a book.

Daddy. Back rigid with anger.

"I know about life, son. I know about sacrifice. I did everything. Everything, to give you and your sister a home. I've done the best I could. I'm not waiting on nobody. I'm not looking at the past. I'm only thinking about the future."

Junior spun around to face Daddy. "Then it's time to let this go!" he said. He grabbed the coffeepot off the counter and slammed it against the kitchen floor. Shards of pointy glass spread out like jagged tears.

Daddy, grabbing Junior by both arms.

Staring him down.

Junior standing his ground. Tears dangling above his cheeks.

Then Daddy, letting go. Sagging like all the air had been let out of him. Even his face sagged.

One minute he was Daddy. The next, he looked as old and tired as his own daddy had before he died and went to Heaven.

A minute passed. The two of them standing there, looking at each other. Daddy turning away, swiping at his face.

Tears?

Not Daddy.

Finally, he said, "Boy, I only meant what was best for you. You and your sister."

Then Junior, voice more plea than rage, said, "You've been waiting on her since she left. Chantel, I mean. You need to move on. Stop living in the past, Pop. Penn State? That was your dream. Chantel coming back, that's your dream, too."

Daddy kept his back to us. When he finally spoke, his voice was as far down the musical scale as you could go. The lowest note of the low.

Gruff. Gravelly.

"A girl needs a mama," he said, nodding toward me.

Junior heaved a big sigh.

"Cady Cat don't need Chantel, Pop. Not when she has me. And you and Fannie and half of Harmony looking out for her," Junior said. He walked around the table until he was face-to-face with Daddy again.

Junior shook his head and said softly, "Let it go. Chantel, the Penn State dream, the memory of what you thought was supposed to happen when you got out of high school, all of it. Let the past go."

Daddy. "What's wrong with Mouse? She's just fine."

Junior. Sounding tired. Not angry. Just tired. "Why do you still call her Mouse?"

Daddy. "'Cause that's what her mama called her. That's her name."

Junior. "Her name is Cadence. She's not a mouse. She hates that name."

Then:

Daddy. "Baby? Is that true? You really hate it when I call you Mouse?"

Me. "Daddy, it's okay. I... It's okay. If that's what you want to call me."

Junior. Shaking his head. Disappointment stretching across his mocha skin.

Daddy. "See? She likes it."

Junior. "Only because she thinks you like it. And you only like it because it gives you one more way to hang on to Chantel."

Then I was no longer among the stars. I was a meteor. Racing. Burning. Shooting across the sky.

Junior staring. Daddy staring. Me crash-landing into my own universe. Me afraid and tired, and tired of being afraid.

"He's right, Daddy," I said. "I hate being called Mouse. Hate it. Hate it, hate it, hate it." The words tumbled out and landed on the floor at my feet, scattering like embers. Or pointy shards of coffeepot glass.

And then...

I drew a breath. Earth continued its orbit. Nothing bad happened. I'd said how I was really feeling, and the Earth continued to orbit the sun.

I kept going. "And the birthday party at the diner? That is not for me. Because I don't want a party at the diner. I want to eat at Chin's with my friends and my family. A real party. Like we used to."

Daddy. "But I thought you loved the diner party. Mouse, really?"

Me. "Daddy, I've only told you like a million times." I went over and hugged him. Tight. I said, "Daddy, Junior, please don't fight anymore. Please?"

All of us. Tired. Feeling bent. Twisted up. But not broken.

Junior, in the kitchen sweeping up the glass shards.

"Sorry, Dad," he said. "I'll replace it."

Daddy. "Don't worry 'bout it, boy. Maybe it is time for a new coffeepot."

I glanced toward the front hall. Daddy saw.

He said, "Ain't nobody leaving, Mou—uh, Cadence. We're all gonna be all right."

15

Hero

One week until my birthday. One day after the ugliest, worst, most awful day of my life. Even worse than the day my mother left. But it was over. Time for church. Daddy and Junior were trying to patch up the ugly with soft words, with Sea Bear jokes, with toast and eggs.

Not perfect. Not yet. There was still so much to say.

Aunt Fannie arrived, and we loaded into the Blueberry. Driving to the Lodge. Junior in the front seat next to Aunt Fannie. Me in the back.

"Let's put some church in this car this morning," Aunt Fannie chirped, cranking up the stereo. Yolanda

Adams, the crowned diva of gospel, her rich, beautiful voice wrapping itself around me.

She sang that many storms have passed your way, and now you feel washed out because life has rained on your parade.

Deeper and deeper I sank into the Blueberry's seats.

Be blessed, don't live life in distress...

The song played on, and when it finished, I asked Aunt Fannie if she'd play it again.

She looked in back at me, and a slow yet concerned smile touched her lips.

"Absolutely, honey bun. Absolutely!"

The rest of the ride, I thought about those lyrics. Not about how to sing them or how wonderful it would be to sound as amazing as Miss Adams.

What I thought about was how accurate the song felt. How when you heard gospel music that touched your soul, it was like having someone turn on a light for you.

I had prayed for God to bless Daddy with a way to buy me a fancy keyboard and microphone. I'd thought getting the instrument would be the blessing I needed, not ever considering that He had already blessed me with a voice and with passion and spirit.

Funny how I'd never really thought about what I had as a gift until Faith wanted me to hand it over to her.

I wish I could say that was the beginning of this big, cosmic turnaround, and after that life got easy-peasy.

It did not get easy-peasy.

Faith was frantic when I entered the Lodge.

"What took you so long? I've sent you about a million texts this morning," she snapped.

"Why?" I asked. I'd been texting with Zara. Her grandmother was doing much better, and Zara expected to come home soon. She was telling me about a trip to an aquarium and how she was positive they had real live mermaids!

So I hadn't answered Faith's messages.

It was then I noticed that for so early in the morning, the Lodge was unusually packed.

"Everybody is here because they think they're going to find out who Gospel Girl is."

I stopped short, almost causing the old man behind me to knock into me and spill his pancakes. "Watch out there, young lady!" he said.

Faith grabbed my elbow and started leading me toward the rehearsal area in back. When we were alone, she started totally freaking out.

"I know I shouldn't have, but I told Mr. Bassie that I was Gospel Girl," she said. "And now the TV people are here!"

"Why would you do that?" I asked, but then I remembered DJ Biscuit and his announcement on the radio yesterday. So much had happened since our visit to State College I'd completely forgotten about the DJ's message.

"I just had to, okay? We were at the church Friday and Saturday for a meeting. My parents were, anyway. I was just there hanging out. Then Jones came in, and you know how he can play piano a little?"

When Faith was nervous she talked very fast. I was trying to keep up.

"So Jones sat down at the piano in the rehearsal room and started to play a little of the song. You know? 'One Sweet Day.' And he said he still didn't think it was me. And I told him it was but I didn't want anybody to know yet, and he kept on saying I didn't want anyone to know because it wasn't true. Then Mr. Bassie came in and saw us, and Jones told him I had something to tell him. . . ."

She stopped, pausing long enough to draw a big breath.

"Then," she said, "it just came out."

"Oh, Faith. Why? Didn't he ask you to sing for him?"

"I told him I was too nervous to do it like that. Then I sort of showed him the video you and I have been working on."

The groan that escaped made my whole body rattle. For days Faith had been coming over to work on the video she wanted to use to scam the church into thinking she was Gospel Girl. I kept telling her I didn't want to do it. Still, she kept pushing. Finally, we made a video that was a perfect lip sync to my singing. We even shot it on my balcony and made it look like how the original video would have looked without help from the app. But Faith had promised not to use it without my okay.

"Faith! How could you?"

She looked around wildly.

"We don't have time for that now. I have an idea. I just need your help."

"Faith! I told you. I'm not going to tell everyone that's really you."

"After all I've done for you over the years, I ask you for one thing, and you're saying no? Please, Mouse? Cadence, please. I'm begging you. Don't let me get humiliated by the TV people. I'll never forgive you if you do!"

"You want me to lie to an entire congregation. In a church," I cried.

"Technically, it's not a church. It's a church brunch. It's entertainment. All I'm asking is for you to help me, um, entertain some folks. Now, come on. Mr. Bassie isn't playing around. He means to have me perform today, and I want to be ready."

Faith's big idea. I mean, really. What was she thinking?

She had found this little nook right off the stage. An area you can't see from the audience and don't really look at if you're onstage. She wanted me to hide in there with a microphone, and we would perform the song just like we'd done on my balcony. Miss Stravinski was going to have the Youth Choir sing backup.

"Faith," I said, after she'd practically run herself crazy, "you have to stop this. I can't do this. Really. I can't."

She moved closer. "You. Have. To. Period!" she growled.

It was official. My very good friend, Faith Bettancourt, had gone insane. I wished with all my heart Zara was with us.

Faith, racing away in a frenzy, reached for a note, but her throat gurgled and her tone snagged like Cinderella's glass slipper after the ball.

Watching her run off, I felt someone standing nearby. I turned to find Jones.

"You don't have to do it, you know," he said. Today his bow tie was candy-apple red with gold-and-green plaid. He wore one of those old-fashioned caps that paperboys used to wear in olden days. His white shirt nearly glowed in the backstage light. I knew the next time I saw him on stage, he'd officially be with the Youth Choir, purple robe and all.

I looked away, smoothing the fabric of my black skirt. "She's my friend," I whispered. "She needs me."

"What about what you need? Don't let her steal your sunshine, girl. Go ahead and be you!"

"But..." I tried to protest.

"But what? C'mon, Mouse."

I looked at him. "I am telling everyone to stop calling me that. I don't like it very much," I said.

"Well, it's about time, *Caaaaaaay-dence*!" he said, stressing the syllables in my name. I laughed, then got serious again.

"This means so much to her, though. And she did make a good point. I'd be pretty hurt if she wrote a best-seller before I did," I said.

Jones looked at me for a minute. He tilted his head to one side and said, "You know I have a reputation for being hard to handle sometimes, right?"

I rolled my eyes, but smiled. "You have a reputation for being a crazy person."

He nodded, smiled back. "Yep! But I'm okay with that. I'm hyper. I jump around a lot. I take medication. Everybody in town knows I'm in foster care. When I was real little and getting bounced around from home to home, I got pitied a lot, too. I got tired of it. Decided if people were going to remember me, it was going to be for something else."

"So you started laughing like a seal?"

He shrugged. "I get good grades. I figured out later on that I could sing. But at the time, acting wild was all I had."

"And now?"

He grinned. "Now I do it because it amuses me! Look, it's good you care about your friends so much. But don't forget to care about you, too."

"But becoming a singing superstar is her big dream. Writing books has always been mine."

In his best Jones fashion, he put both hands on his hips and scowled at me from beneath the brim of his plaid hat and said, "Oh? And you can't have TWO dreams?"

Just then, Miss Stravinski started calling for places.

Jones shrugged. "Gotta go. I'm singing the duet with her. I mean, with Gospel Girl. See you onstage." He winked and dashed off.

♫ ♫ ♫

Mr. Bassie was in rare form. The scent of fresh-baked waffles and coffee and cream filled the room. Anticipation was thicker than maple syrup.

While Miss Stravinski had been collecting us all to take the stage, I'd hidden in the tiny alcove Faith had picked out. The microphone was clipped to the collar of my white shirt. It was like this movie I saw a couple years ago called *The Parent Trap*, about twins who were separated when they were little and play a trick on their divorced parents.

Only instead of twins and summer camp and California and England, you've got a scaredy-mouse and a superstar!

"How's everybody doing this morning?" Mr. Bassie asked. He wore a beautiful navy blue suit with a white, blue, and purple pocket square sticking out of his front pocket. A pale lavender shirt with a navy-and-white tie made the whole look stand out. When I glanced across the stage, I spotted Aunt Fannie. She wore her robe and was looking longingly at Mr. Bassie.

I felt a sudden heart pang for her. I had no idea how the Husband Pageant was going. Was she in the lead, or had she been forced to drop out?

Aunt Fannie was so different from my mother. The ugly words that had spilled on our kitchen floor and made our house feel foreign, Junior calling my mother selfish, kept replaying in my mind.

I had tried to never think of my mother that way. Never. Yet, I knew, somewhere deep down, that was exactly how I saw her. She'd left us. Just walked out. Part of me wanted to understand that she did it for her "art."

But, honestly, when I grow up, if I have a little girl—or even a boy—I hope I never have to leave their side. I hope to be there, loving them and caring for them. Just like my daddy.

Then I thought of Aunt Fannie again. No matter how she was doing in the Husband Pageant, she wouldn't just leave us. Or me.

Like Auntie, I didn't want to be selfish. But I didn't want to be pushed around, either.

The music started. I caught Faith staring in my direction. Mr. Bassie stood center stage. His smile was an ocean. His eyes twinkled. He rapped the microphone with his long fingers and said, "Let's put our hands together for Harmony's own Gospel Girl, Miss Faith Bettancourt!"

The whole thing unfolded in slow motion.

Jones went to stand beside Faith as the applause was dying down.

How had I let this happen?

Why hadn't I flat-out refused?

Faith looked worse than afraid. She looked wretched. She had to know this was a crazy idea.

How had I let things get so out of control?

Jones began:

Sorry, I never told you
All I wanted to say....

His voice was rich, controlled, full of emotion. He made each note believable, each syllable necessary. His verse finished, and the music swirled around him.

Faith's eyes darted side to side. She looked frantic. Trapped.

I couldn't lie anymore.

I'd made a promise. I promised God if He made my wish come true, I'd be better. Stronger. My prayer, I realized, hadn't just been about getting a fancy keyboard or having the confidence to sing in front of others. I'd made a deal to use the blessing He'd given me and share it to shine a light on those who needed it. It was my deal with the Almighty. Not Faith's. Not anyone else's.

And it was something I needed to do for me, too.

People in the audience had begun to look around.

Miss Stravinski played on.

Mr. Bassie looked . . . at me. Soon as our gazes touched, it was clear.

He knew.

I ran onto the stage, beside Faith. I put her between Jones and me.

"Ladies and gentlemen, I believe we've got someone here with something to tell us. Is that right, Miss Jolly?" Mr. Bassie said with a wink. What was with all the winking? First, Jones. Now Mr. Bassie. *Honestly!*

Even in the glare from the lights, I could see Junior standing at the edge of the stage.

And beside him was Daddy.

He looked so confused. *Oh, boy!*

Daddy hadn't been to the Lodge on a Sunday since my mother left. Well, at least this would save me the trouble of having to break it to him later.

"Hi, everybody," I mumbled into the microphone on the stand.

"*SPEAK UP!*" shouted the crowd. I did something wrong with the mic, and it squawked.

I cringed. My heart was beating far too fast. The lights felt too warm. The walls were pushing together, and I feared I was going to get squished.

Jones reached over, grabbed one hand. He said, "You can do it, girl!"

Faith chewed her lip. She looked close to tears. "I'm sorry, Mou... *Cadence*."

The thumping in my chest threatened to push me off the stage. But I'd gone too far to turn around now.

I hugged Faith and said into the microphone, "Everybody, first let me say thank you to my friend, Faith. She just did this because she knew I was the one who..."

Deep breath. This was it. God, I sure hope this counts as keeping my promise.

"I was the one who recorded the Gospel Girl video. She knew I was too shy to ever come out on my own. Faith is a real friend!"

Applause. Jones nudged me; Faith gave me a hug.

I continued, my voice breaking, "I—I made the video thinking only Mr. Bassie and Miss Stravinski would see it. But, like he said a few weeks ago, it accidentally went viral. But sometimes I guess things happen for a reason."

"AMEN!" shouted the room.

I leaned over and whispered a question to Jones. He nodded his head in agreement. I said, "I know you all are expecting me to do the song that got me into this mess." Everyone laughed. I went on. "But I'd like to do a song my aunt sang a few weeks ago. And I'd like her to join me. Aunt Fannie, would you please help me out?"

She came onto the stage, with a flourish, of course. I'd asked Jones if he'd mind letting me sing with Auntie. "As long as I get to sing with you next time," he'd whispered back, before running, doing a leap and a twirl to a chorus of "JONES!" before getting off the stage.

Aunt Fannie was beaming. She gave me a big hug. "Oh, sugar pie. I've been waiting for this day for so long. The day when I could sing with my perfect little angel. My niece!"

That brought a tear to my eye.

How long had I been waiting and hoping to write a perfect ending for the story of me, center stage and sharing the moment with the woman who'd loved me for so many years? In the story I'd wanted to write, that woman had been my mother. Yet, here was someone I loved deeply, who'd been here the whole time.

Aunt Fannie stood opposite Faith, and Miss Stravinski gave the piano bench to Mr. Bassie. He began the opening chords to "Anytime You Need a Friend," the song Aunt Fannie had brought down the house with a few weeks back.

She began, singing flawlessly. When she turned to me, I could feel every person in the room sucking in air.

I exhaled and released the next line. It sounded off, like the notes were leaning to one side. Aunt Fannie moved closer, placed her arm around me, and I felt her warmth through the robe.

"*Anytime you need a friend*," we sang together in the chorus, our words blossoming together like prize roses in the sunshine. I couldn't believe I was doing it, either. Singing. At some point, I stopped thinking altogether. I just closed my eyes, and I sang. And the words went round-trip, from Earth to Heaven, from Heaven to Earth.

And I thought about the keyboard that had meant so much to me. The instrument I was sure I needed to get the confidence to stand tall and sing. Musical notes rolled out, climbing the scale, higher and higher. People stood, cheered. Gave me love, and I gave it right back.

And I knew that I'd possessed the instrument I needed all along.

I had the voice God gave me.

Applause grew frenzied, pierced with shrieks and whistles, sending my soul higher than my voice as the notes and scales carried us. Aunt Fannie, whose voice was magically powerful, allowed me to shine, supporting me when I needed it, pulling back when I was ready to stand on my own.

I could not have asked for anything else.

It was the best day ever.

And I did NOT have to make it up!

16

Butterfly

And we lived happily ever after!

Well, not exactly. After church that day, Daddy, Aunt Fannie, Junior, and I came back to the house and sat down and talked.

Really talked.

Daddy asked once again if I'd really hated being called Mouse. *Oh, Daddy. Of course I hate it.* I told him in the most delicate way that Mouse was the absolute worst, most miserable nickname a future girl of power and ambition could ever have.

"No one wants a book autographed by a writer named Mouse. They really, truly don't," I said.

He held out his hand and said, "Pleasure to make your acquaintance, Cadence."

I gave him a punch in the arm. The kind of thing he and Junior did to each other. I'd never really punched anyone. It kinda hurt my knuckles. But I didn't even say ouch. I wanted Daddy to start thinking of me as a girl who could be strong.

"My . . . I mean, Mom, she had another nickname for me. She said she wanted to call me Moon Goddess or Luna, Goddess of the Moon. I like that," I said.

Junior snorted. "More like Looney-toon!"

"Hush, Junior." Aunt Fannie snapped a towel at him.

We all laughed. Daddy said, "Nice to meet you, Moon Goddess."

Aunt Fannie kept hugging me, and I'd catch her glancing over at me, too. Apparently she had a lot to say. About how much she adored me and wanted what was best for me, how she hated to see me cooped up waiting and hoping for the return of a woman who was not willing to put her life on hold for me or the rest of our family. It was hard to hear—for me and Daddy, too, but I couldn't say I disagreed.

Still, I was nervous when I asked, "Daddy, are you going to stop seeing Miss Clayton?"

He sighed, then said, "I . . . it's time for me to move on. Your mama has her life. I think it's time for me to have mine, too."

He was his goofy old self, all big hands and big head and soft brown eyes. He looked at me. "I didn't want to turn you against your mother. I loved her so much. Love you so much. I just wanted what was best for you," he said.

I grinned. Not a shy grin, either. Wide and proud. "Daddy! You are what's good for me. And Miss Clayton is nice."

"She is," he said. Now he was smiling again.

Junior was leaning against the kitchen counter eating one of the chicken wings out of the basket of wings Aunt Fannie was cooking. "If you need some pointers on how to keep your lady happy, old man, I'll hook you up," Junior said.

Daddy laughed and shook his head. "You wait till you get up to Michigan. Those girls over there are going to be too smart to fall for your nonsense. Wait and see," Daddy said.

The two of them had made up. Well, sort of. Neither of them apologized. They just did what men do, I guess—they shook hands, called each other goofy names, then watched football together. Living with Daddy and Junior, I'd learned that almost anything could be settled between men with football. And the right snacks.

When I asked Aunt Fannie how she was doing with Mr. Bassie, she smiled. "I think he might be sweet on that Letitia Jenkins," she said. *Oh, no!* Letitia Jenkins was the woman at church whose skirts looked like they were made for the dance clubs on Saturday nights instead of the church pews on Sunday mornings. At least, that was what I'd overheard a few of the old women at church saying.

"She lacks your sophistication," I said loyally.

Aunt Fannie grinned. "She does, indeed," she said. "However, Garrett McEntyre, you know him? The butcher? Well, he asked me out on a date, and I said yes."

The butcher! I thought he was scared of her flourishes!

She showed me how to make a piecrust and asked a million questions about books and the kinds of stories I wanted to write. She also told me how lonely she'd been and how much joy she got from being with us and teaching me things after my mother left.

I'd never thought about Aunt Fannie being a single lady with no children and living alone. She always seemed so busy and full of life. She told me she stayed busy to keep from feeling sorry for herself. She said she'd love to have a little girl to dress and teach and love.

I told her I might know just the right girl. Someone very close, indeed.

School was ridiculous. But at least Zara was back.

"Gran is so much better, Luna!" she exclaimed. We had texted back and forth. She was up to date on the madness.

Our classroom was crazy. Everybody kept coming up to me, telling me how surprised they were to learn that I was Gospel Girl. It was hard for a while.

Having so many people coming at me, talking, looking at me. I felt myself dip underwater, bubbles floating around, my heart rate speeding, hard to breathe, time slowing down.

However, when I looked around, I realized, much like in the song I'd sung with Auntie at the Lodge, even when I was drowning, or felt like I was drowning, I wasn't alone.

Zara, my favorite mermaid, was there. And Faith, our reigning barracuda, was by my side, too.

Then I felt a tiny flutter in my chest. A tingle that slowly spread throughout my body. *Anytime you need a friend…*

I had gotten what I'd prayed for, and I'd made good on my promise. Knowing that was the best feeling in the whole entire world.

Tuesday morning.

At six thirty I sat with Faith, Jones, and Aunt Fannie in what was called the greenroom. And the walls weren't even green.

It was the studio for Channel Eight. *Good Morning, Western Pennsylvania.*

"Auntie," I whispered, "I don't think I can do it."

"You can do it, baby. Auntie is right here. The minute I think it's too much for you, I'll grab you up in my arms and sweep you out of here."

Daddy sat across from us. Junior, too.

The two of them were still fussing about schools. I saw Junior kept trying to put a Michigan baseball cap on Daddy. Junior didn't realize Daddy had stuck an I ♥ PENN STATE sticker on his back.

Both of them were grinning. I sighed. What if grown-up men were just like Junior and his high school friends? Oh, I didn't even want to think about a thing like that!

When it was time to be interviewed, a girl smelling like hair spray and cigarette smoke came and clipped portable microphones on us and led us onto a stage. We were seated next to the show's host, a woman named Bonnie Smythe.

"Good day, western PA! We have with us here today a young lady who exploded onto the Internet music scene just a few short weeks ago. Her identity had been disguised, causing quite a stir. Now this future gospel star has come out of hiding and is none other than Harmony's own Miss *Candace* Jolly!"

The woman's smile was wide and slippery. Who could wear so much makeup so early in the morning?

"Cadence!" Faith was saying.

The woman looked confused.

"Excuse me, dear?" Her smile looked plastered on.

Faith, once again, had decided to jump in. I placed my hand on her arm. It was time I learned to take care of myself. In my own way.

My voice was softer, and my manner was less brash. I didn't always like it. But I was learning that part of the responsibility for growing up was being willing to take action for yourself. I mean, I was about to turn eleven.

So I sat up a little higher in the seat. Forced a smile onto my very frightened lips, and said, "Good morning, Miss Bonnie. My name isn't CAN-dace, though. It's Cadence."

I smiled.

She smiled.

In six minutes, it was all over.

"... happy birthday to yooooooooooooou!"

Honk! Snort. Honk! Snort. Honk! Snort. Honk! Snort.

We were seated in the back of Chin's Chinese Restaurant. Mei-Mei was there, along with Jones, Faith, Zara, and Sophie.

Faith was pressed next to me, whispering, "You have to write a book about all of this. Just think. It would be amazing. And I want to be your agent!"

When we left the television station, we'd gone directly back to school. However, by lunchtime, so many kids wanted to talk about us being on the morning show and what happened in church that the principal decided we were too much of a distraction. She "invited" our parents to let us go home early and have the afternoon off.

Faith came back home with me, and we wound up reading one of the books that Sofine had given me: *The School Story*, by Andrew Clements.

It's about this girl who wants to be a writer, like me. And her mom works for a publisher. And the girl's friend reads her novel and thinks it's genius. So the friend decides to act as the agent, and they try to get her book published.

And the best thing about it?

Their teacher, the one who helps them out, her name is Miss Clayton. Speaking of Miss Clayton, she was sitting on the opposite end of the long table from Daddy, but I'd caught them more than once making eyes at each other. Very good, indeed.

Anyway, since we read the book, Faith has been begging me to write a story about everything that had happened with us over the past four weeks.

"You guys know what?" Jones said. "Just three more weeks till the Jamboree!"

My first feeling was guilt; I'd been too afraid to audition the right way so I'd be stuck with the kiddie choir for the performance. Then the fear factor sent a warning shot to my brain.

OH, NO! Only three weeks until the Jamboree! Even as part of the kiddie choir there'd be lots of work to do.

And what would happen now that everyone knew I could actually sing? Would I need to lead a song? Would Little Precious try to scratch my eyes out? What was going to happen?

Sophie must have seen me turning green. She came over and demanded, "Oh, no. You will not spoil your party by freaking out. Not today. Eat cake and dance!" And so we did.

Daddy had canceled the party at the diner. He told Sofine he wanted just a small gathering. A few family members and friends. I liked that.

Even so, a curious number of people had "just decided" they wanted to have dinner at Chin's, too.

Out of nowhere, the Trinity appeared behind me. Eeeek! Was I going to get Trinitied again?

The three church ladies moved as one. Each dressed in blue, varying shades from ocean blue to sky blue to the blue of ink. Each wore a hat that presented a beautiful feather plume, peacock style.

Miss Lily said, "We are all so very proud of you, Little Miss Lady."

"Very proud," echoed Miss Wanda.

Sister Dahlia reached out for me, and I felt my body tense. Something about getting prayed over by the Trinity Sisters gave me the shakes.

However, instead of praying on me like they were healing me, Miss Wanda said, "We heard about you canceling the big to-do at the diner on account of wanting to spend time with your friends and family."

Sister Dahlia: "Friends and family, hallelujah!"

Miss Lily nodded, and Miss Wanda continued. "But we wanted you to know that sharing your birthday with you and your family over the years has been a blessing for all of us. And we thank you for sharing that with us."

Each one of them hugged me, and I was too surprised to speak.

"And we wanted you to have this, now that you are sure to become a woman of great notice someday," said Sister Dahlia, producing a fat, square box.

"Please open it!" Miss Wanda said.

So I did.

Inside, buried beneath a field of brightly colored tissue paper, sat a hat. My very own church lady hat.

"Consider yourself an honorary member of our little sisterhood," Miss Lily said. After that, it seemed like the right time for presents. I couldn't believe what the ladies had said—that allowing them to throw the parties had been a blessing for them, too.

I was still thinking about that when I noticed that Sofine had entered the restaurant. She came over, kissed me on the cheek.

"I'm not going to interrupt your festivities," she said. Tonight her lipstick was bright pink, and her beehive was a glossy black, encircled with a wreath of white flowers.

"I just wanted to say happy birthday, sugar. And I wanted to give you a little something."

She pushed a package at me, and everyone yelled, "Open it!"

So I did. It was a small red purse. No. Not a purse. It was a small book bag.

She grinned. "Just room enough for one book and maybe a few mint tea bags."

Strangely enough, I felt my eyes sting with tears. I blinked them back as I looked into Sofine's smiling face. She frowned, then gathered me to her.

"Oh, shucks, baby. Now, no need for tears. You know I was happy to do it," she said, pulling back to look at me once again. When I looked at her, I saw the same concerned face, the same smiling eyes that took in everything from my hair to my clothes to my mood. She'd always given me those things willingly, and I'd accepted them grudgingly. Now I looked around the room, saw it filling with people who were "coincidentally" having dinner at Chin's on the night of my birthday.

Another astronomy word crossed my mind. *Aurora.* It means a bright glow. Which was exactly how it felt to be so truly blessed.

"Really, Sofine," I whispered against her shoulder, "thank you. With all my heart!" She squeezed me one last time, then rushed off, maybe afraid she might tear up, too.

When the rest of the presents came out, I received several Mariah-inspired gifts. For example, I got a charm bracelet, in honor of an old album of hers with the same name.

And Faith gave me a beautiful gold butterfly charm.

"You know, because you like her song 'Butterfly' so much," she said.

Junior upgraded my iPod to an even better one. And he'd already added a bigger song list.

"Check it out, Cady Cat. I think it's time you spread out beyond your Mariah obsession. I got you some Mary Mary, some Kim Burrell, Yolanda Adams—all great women of gospel. There's some pop music in there, too. Taylor Swift, Katy Perry, Keyshia Cole. Even a few country songs. Time for you to stretch your mind, little sister," he said.

"I got you a little something, too," said Auntie. When I opened her box, I gasped.

"Are they real?" I said.

"Absolutely. I thought maybe you'd like to move up from your genuine imitation pearls and have the real thing," she said.

A beautiful, delicate string of pearls sat on a bed of cotton. I hugged Auntie so hard I almost toppled us.

"Thank you, Auntie. For the pearls, for everything," I whispered.

When she shook off the tears threatening to fall, you know she did it with a flourish!

♫♬♫

Daddy saved his gift for last.

When we got home, he said, "I had this done while we were out. Watch your step."

He made me cover my eyes with my hand and led me up the steps to the third floor. Something smelled weird, but I wasn't sure what it was. I could hear Daddy and Junior trying to whisper about something.

What was it?

Then I felt a door open. Daddy nudged me forward and told me to open my eyes.

It took a moment for my eyes to adjust.

My bedroom.

Fresh paint.

No more calming blue.

Now it was exciting pink, with dashes of yellow and intriguing red. Not just the walls. The curtains, bedspread, even the rug. Even Lyra's bow tie was red.

"It's what you want, Cadence. This is for you. I love you, kiddo!"

I love you, too, Daddy.

♫ ♫ ♫

One more thing…

A little while later that night, Daddy called me downstairs. He had checked the messages on the phone.

There was a message for me.

"Happy birthday, baby. It's me. Mom. I wish I could have been there. I saw you and Fannie singing together on the news. Oh, Mouse, you were great. I'm going to leave a number where I'll be tonight. Call me when you get in. I want to hear all about your night. I tried calling your cell phone, but your voice mail was full. Love you so much, Mouse. Miss you!"

Daddy looked at me. "Want to call her back?"

I thought for a second. I'd been waiting so long for that phone call. I'd thought I needed it more than anything. Thought without it, I might never find the strength to be me.

Turned out, I had all the strength I needed. I reached inside my pocket and fished out my phone. I handed it to Daddy.

"Maybe we can call her tomorrow," I said. "I'm tired."

Daddy looked uncertain. "You know how your mama is. She may not be at that number tomorrow."

I turned my palms up. "Oh, well..." I said.

"Good night, Cadence, my little Moon Goddess. I've got to get used to calling you that. What about Moony G?"

"G'night, Sea Bear!"

"Oh, by the way, Mr. Bassie called before we went out."

I turned back to look at him. A question mark between my brows. "What did he want?"

Daddy, being his usual too-playful self, grinned. "I dunno. Something about you and your friends being able to consider yourselves part of the Youth Choir starting next week. I'm not sure. I told him y'all weren't interested, but—"

"Daddy!" He really could be aggravating. "You play too much!" I laughed, shaking my head.

"Congratulations, Moon Doggy!"

"Goddess. But you can call me Luna. You can call me Cadence. You can call me whatever you want. But please, never, ever call me Mouse!"

♫ ♫ ♫

Underneath the quilted night sky, I sat on the balcony breathing in sweet, sugary air filled with snowflakes as bright as falling stars. Lyra was on my lap, licking my face. I held up my iPad.

"Look, girl! I have something to show you!" I said.

Lyra was the perfect dog for a future bestselling author. Curious. Considerate. And she asked just the right questions.

I turned on my tablet, then tabbed through my favorite videos. I'd reset them recently. I scrolled past one after another. Then I came to what I was looking for. Joya Booker from church. She had started posting her videos. I watched how she was with the choir. I was getting pointers. After all, my friends and I were officially in the Youth Choir now.

The feeling was so wonderful. I looked into the sky, waved to a point far above the stars.

"Thank you, God! Sorry about trying to skip out on my promise. Thank you for blessing me and my family."

I went inside after that and tried really hard not to start worrying about the upcoming Gospel Jamboree.

Or having to sing with the big kids.

Or about what might happen between Daddy and Miss Clayton.

As I drifted off to sleep, I realized that learning to be strong didn't mean changing everything. I curled into Lyra and snuggled into her warm snores. In the key of G.

ACKNOWLEDGMENTS

My aunts, Gladys Winston and Sue Anderson, both passed away while I was writing this book. It is an unbelievable loss for our family. And so, in loving memory of two great old gals, I'd like to dedicate this book to them. Their spirit for life, their laughter, and gifts for storytelling and good times played key roles in the creation of certain characters. May God bless.

Also, I would like dedicate this book to my late agent, George Nicholson. He was the driving force behind this project. Normally stoic and oh-so-cosmopolitan, it was rare to see him awed. But when I introduced the idea over lunch in a Manhattan bistro one sunny summer day, he became downright effusive. "You must write this, my dear!" he declared. He died before the project was completed, but it was his voice I heard quietly pushing me along the way. I miss you, George. I miss you and my aunties. God bless.

Thirdly, this novel is dedicated to the buoyant spirit of Mariah Carey's music, especially her early hits, which played a huge role in my life. Warbling along with her fiercely emotional or effervescently upbeat tunes helped me conquer demons and slay dragons, feel love and sharpen creativity. You've inspired me, Miss Mariah. Your musical gifts helped shape this story and give it life. Thank you!

It takes a lot of good hearts and strong minds to put together a book. Super-duper thanks to the lady who makes me—and my books—look good, designer Marcie Lawrence. Special acknowledgment to my editor, Allison Moore, who knows how to inspire the best in me, all the while making me believe it was my idea. And thank you, Esther Cajahuaringa, for being a kick-butt intern at

Little, Brown Books for Young Readers and a great supporter of my work.

And lastly, a thank-you to the community that raised me in the spirit of gospel music. You helped bring Cadence and her world to life.

Turn the page for a preview of

AVAILABLE NOW

1

Declaration of Independence!

My name is Brianna Justice, and I want to be president of the whole fifth grade!

That is my "declaration."

As in, "I do declare that *I will be president* of the whole entire fifth grade at Orchard Park Elementary."

My aunt Tina says that if we want good things to happen we have to make them happen. Take action! State your plan out loud. **DECLARE!**

And I want good things to happen. I have BIG plans. I'm going to be a millionaire with my own cooking show on TV. Cupcakes are my specialty.

Aunt Tina also says that along with declaring your goal, you have to have a plan. Think about what you want, decide how you plan to get it, then write it down and keep notes along the way. That's how you make a plan. All really important, successful people do, she says. (Grandpa says if Aunt Tina had a husband instead of "just a career" maybe she wouldn't have time for so many plans. *Hmph!*) Anyway, ever since a certain hometown celebrity spoke to our class last January, I've known what I need to do. Here's my plan:

I live in Orchard Park, Michigan. We're not far from Detroit, Michigan. But Orchard Park is a suburb. That means unless you live here, you probably never heard of it. At least, not until my hero, Miss Delicious, became world-famous as a chef, author, TV-show host, and GAZILLIONAIRE. Miss Delicious grew up right here in Orchard Park.

And she even went to the same elementary school as me!

When she spoke to our fourth-grade class, she told us that she didn't think any of her success would have been possible had it not been for the skills she learned at our school.

But this is the most important thing she said:

"I honestly believe that if I hadn't been voted president of my fifth-grade class, if I hadn't learned how to manage my responsibilities back then and be a true leader, I don't know if any of this would have been possible."

So the best way for me to follow in her footsteps would be to become president of my fifth-grade class, too.

Ever since that day, every morning when I arrive at school, I pass through the front hallway where all the plaques hang or sit on shelves showing the names of all the fifth graders who have been president. And I say a tiny little prayer and run my fingers over Miss Delicious's name for good luck.

That same day I told my friends, basically our whole class, that I was going to be just like Miss Delicious. I was going to be a millionaire cupcake baker and sell tons of books and be wildly famous on television.

And the first step would be to become president of the fifth grade.

So you see, it is so totally obvious: I have to win the election.

All summer I planned. I've written speeches. I've

researched school-approved places for our class trip and other interests vital to our fifth-grade class.

Little did I know how much would change once school started up after summer break. My plan seemed to be going so well, *until*…

2

"The Redcoats Are Coming..."

... *Until!*

A tiny word, but it can be an ugly thing.

Like the way parents use it:

"No chocolate cake *until* you finish your broccoli." Or... "No allowance *until* all your chores are finished!" Or "You did what? Just wait *until* I tell your father, missy!"

See what I mean? *Until.* It's not hard to spell, but when it crashes into a kid's life, it can really wreck her day.

What had happened was: I was all set to take my rightful place in history as fifth-grade president at Orchard Park Elementary. Mrs. Nutmeg had asked the class to nominate the student or students worthy of being president. My friends nominated me and almost the whole class seconded it. Except the disgusting Back Row Boys. We had all known that Todd Hampton's fellow toadies would nominate him. *Hmph!* Like he could really win. He was still acting funky because while I was planning and plotting and waiting for my chance at the school elections, I took an afternoon off this summer to kick his butt in basketball. That's right. My all-girl team beat his all-boy team. It felt so good, I made up my own song:

Ah, ha, okay! The girls are better any day!

Yeah, I love that song. Todd, not so much.

So of course he was going to run against me, and of course he had no shot because, let's face it, everybody, Everybody, EVERYBODY knows I'm much better prepared than Todd and would make a much better president.

Except there was a new twist—the election wasn't just for each fifth-grade class to have its own president. Nuh-uh. This year, for the first time in Orchard Park Elementary history, there would be only ONE fifth-grade president.

President of the WHOLE fifth grade.

But the twists didn't stop there! Now, this year, not

only would the winner of the election be president of the whole fifth grade, he or she would be president of the whole school. If that wasn't enough to throw me for a loop, Dr. Beelie had won some kind of grant, which is a fancy teacher way of saying money—cash, moola, cheddar, ching-ching. So the new school president and president of the whole fifth grade would also have a HUGE responsibility: deciding how to use the $5,000 budget. Five thousand smackeroonies! The idea of being in charge of that kind of money made me light-headed with happiness.

My heart leapt at the news. Back when Miss Delicious spoke at our school, I thought I could be president of just my class, same as it had always been. But now that had changed. Was I ready for that big of a challenge? That kind of responsibility?

I couldn't help thinking about other challenges, other goals I'd had. Like the time I decided I needed to be the best free-throw shooter on our team. I'd written down my notes on how to stand, how to breathe, stuff coach had talked to me about, and stuff Dad helped me find online. That had been an important goal for me. And I did it!

So was I ready to be school president and president of the whole fifth grade?

YES! Yes, I was.

So bring it on. It would be even better than I had imagined. And I could just see me making my acceptance speech, that is, *until*...

Mrs. Gayle entered our classroom with a girl whose long, crinkly hair almost covered her face and said the words that will haunt me forever and ever. Mrs. Gayle said:

"Everyone, we have a new student. Please say hello to Jasmine Moon..."

ELECTION NOTEBOOK

(Mrs. Nutmeg says all of her students need to keep some kind of journal about the school elections, especially the candidates!)

Election Rules

- *Each* of the five fifth-grade classes will have to pick two students. If more than two students get picked in one classroom, they have to have a mini-election called a "primary" to choose which two will run.

- When each class has its two picks or candidates for president, those students compete against each other and all the other candidates. Whoever gets the most votes from kids from first grade to fifth grade wins!

- The winner gets to go to Washington, D.C., to tour the *White House*, Principal Beelie told us.

- What could be a better way to learn leadership skills and launch a mega-million-dollar empire than to be president of all the grades and all the kids at your school and go to the real White House?

Don't miss Sherri Winston's other amazing books.

BOB850

STORIES ABOUT FRIENDSHIP, GROWING UP, AND FINDING YOURSELF!

Sherri Winston

is the author of *President of the Whole Fifth Grade* (a Sunshine State Young Readers Award selection), *President of the Whole Sixth Grade* (a Kids' Indie Next pick), *President of the Whole Sixth Grade: Girl Code*, and *The Kayla Chronicles*. She lives with her family in Florida. Her website is voteforcupcakes.com.